# SHADES

A.L. HAWKE

PHANTOM HEART, LLC

Line edited by Stephanie Marshall Ward

Proofread by Alexa B.

Cover Design © 2023 by Regina Wamba of MaeIDesign.com

Published by Phantom Heart, LLC

27702 Crown Valley Pkwy, Suite D4, #201

Ladera Ranch, CA 92694

Printed and bound in the United States of America

First printing February, 2023

Learn more about A.L. Hawke at www.alhawke.com

Correspondence: contact@alhawke.com

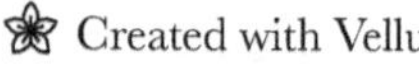 Created with Vellum

*For my father*
*For the love of cars and the search for meaning*

**1**

—————

# ALMOST LIKE AN ANGEL

HE SHUFFLED HIS DUSTY BOOTS ALONG THE MUD AND gravel. Yesterday it had rained, and there were still a few wisps of white and gray dispersed over an otherwise clear violet sky, but it was mostly clear now. This was his treasured spot. His sanctuary. On the infinite horizon, orange and red spread over vast distances of scattered weeds and shrubs, while behind him was darkness. He tore his eyes from the view and looked down at a drop of at least three hundred feet below. His fingers fidgeted in the pockets of his worn black leather jacket as he gazed down from the precipice. Then, as the sun rose, he removed his shades and stared out again.

"Angel down," said the voice on his cell phone. "Amanda. Twenty-two. A blond college graduate. English major. She's looking for a job in journalism. Born a Pisces. She's rooming in an apartment with an Asian student in Santa Monica. Now she's at the border by Arizona. Where are you at, John?"

"Not far from there."

He turned, facing the dark clouds of Los Angeles.

"The girl's off on some road trip, John. We have no

idea where the hell she's going. Or why. Just intercept her. Get over there before Lilith does."

"Send me the location."

He turned back to the desert horizon. The yellow sun rose. It blinded his naked eyes, but he liked that. He withstood the pain from the burning light. He let the light wash over his face and body. Then a silhouette of a bird soared on the horizon, perhaps a few miles from where he stood. It was deep in the desert in the middle of nowhere. Like him, it seemed to wander without direction. Its wingtips touched wisps of the bright light of the sun, almost like an angel.

## 2

# RESPLENDENT

"Guys, you know, I mean, what can I say? How can I describe this? Breathtaking? Check. Amazing? Check. Incredible? How 'bout resplendent? That's what the desert is. Resplendent." She laughed, remembering the word from an essay for her English Lit final. "I tell you guys, it's positively resplendent."

A perfect orange and red painted horizon opened up before her after she ascended an incline, while weeds and saguaros rushed by her, on both sides of her green VW, seemingly stretching forever in a stunning, endless desert vista. She pressed the record button on her old handheld recorder again.

"I wish you could be here with me. The sun's rising, the trees are gone, replaced by cacti the size of people, and behind me are LA's ugly rain clouds and smog, which I'm happy to be leaving behind. It's like nature's opening up and it's as excited as I am to be here. Hello, nature. Hello.

"The furthest I've ever driven in my life is Vegas and Portland, so everything is new. That's what I'm gonna bring to you. New. Fresh. And resplendent." She chuckled again. "I'm bringing resplendent to you all right now..." She leaned forward, gazing at the horizon. "God, it's beautiful. Spiny cactus. Yeah, spiny everywhere for miles. And the soil's changed too. It's getting red. Red! *Can you believe that!*

"So, Amanda?

"Hey, what's up?"

"What's the first thing you're going to do after you graduate from college?

"Hmm... I don't know? How 'bout travel across the country?"

*Like really travel.*

Sunlight blinked between saguaros outside her window. Then, after another short incline, was the infinite desert horizon again.

"What do you hope to find a thousand miles away from home?"

"A tall, dark, and handsome man... Rest stops. Slushies."

She nodded, clicked the stop button, and stuffed the recorder back in her pants pocket. That was enough.

Then she tapped her fingers on the steering wheel, gazing over her green hood as the voice of Steve Perry sang "You Better Wait." The song seemed perfect for the start of her trip. She touched the glass. Chilly. Well, not for long. It was going to get hot later. Then she glanced at her sole companion, vibrating in the passenger seat—a small, prickly cactus in a clay planter she'd just bought at a gas station, her first souvenir. Then she accompanied Steve Perry like a total dork in a loud sing-along of "You Better Wait"—until her speakers were interrupted by the ringing of her cell phone.

"Mands," said a voice in her car speaker. "Hey Mands, you still alive out there?"

Amanda leaned forward again, watching a bird with wide-stretched wings soar over her car on the two-lane free-way. Behind its wings sprawled the vista of that orange-red streak. It was so much like a painting. So beautiful. The bird passed from view above the car.

"I just left, dummy," Amanda said. She looked down at the console. "Hey, guess what, Lu?"

"What's up?"

"I started my podcast."

"O-k-a-y."

"I thought you liked my podcasts?"

"Course I do. I'm your number one fan."

"Yeah. You know what I called the desert? Resplendent. Absolutely resplendent. Isn't *resplendent* a great word?"

"You're so freaky, Mands," she said with a laugh. "I love you."

"Love you too. So what's up?"

"Ben called." Luane laughed.

"That's early."

"Yeah, he said it's because he couldn't stop thinking 'bout me since last night. Can you believe that? I played it down. But I kept thinking of him standing over me, reaching down and gently touching my lips. God, Mands, Benji's so hot. He told me he was going to be working near Big Bear over the summer. I thought the mountains was all about skiing and snow. You know, it's the snow I love. He said he'll be running some sort of bike shop up there and he wanted me to come up. I thought we can visit together. If you don't get kidnapped in Texas or something."

Amanda headed down another incline but still, far off, she could see an infinite horizon with the rising yellow-red sun. She looked up, but her bird was gone.

"It gets really hot in the summer in the mountains," Amanda said.

"It gets hot everywhere in the summer. I sure hope so…'round Ben."

There it was. The large bird was hovering in the sky, easily visible now. It just floated. But it must have been gliding fast. Amanda was barreling down the highway at eighty-five miles per hour. She wondered if she was like this bird—like a bird flying without direction. That's what she was like this morning.

"Pretty."

"More like handsome," Luane said.

"Not Benji. It's just so pretty out here. I wish you could see it with me, Lu."

"I hate road trips. So here's the thing. If I go with Ben to the mountains, I won't be in LA. So—"

"How long will you be gone?"

"You don't get it. I want you to come with me, Mandi. Want to? It'd be so much fun! Benji said he has a few cabins up there that'll be free for us to use. We can spend some time up there free of charge and bike, you know."

"I don't know. I thought we'd hang by the beach."

"Well, the beach is expensive. I can get us a cabin for free for a few months until we're done interviewing. But I need to know, like, *now*. He said he's stalling and someone else wants it."

Amanda lost sight of her bird again. It had faded off the desert horizon.

"So? What do you say?"

"Big Bear?"

"Or Arrowhead. I'm not really sure. Something in that direction. Yeah."

"It wouldn't take me long to visit you even if I stayed in LA."

"Except you won't 'cause you're coming with me."

Amanda laughed. "Okay, let me think about it." She looked at the small cactus vibrating in her passenger seat. "Hey, whatever happens, I'm bringing you a new friend. He's smaller than Benji, but he's just as prickly."

"What do you mean?"

"It's a cactus. Your boyfriends are always prickly like that."

"That's my cue to tell you to go fuck off. Mandi, love ya and all, but I have to know. Can we stay up there or not?"

Amanda said nothing. She wickedly loved the silence, knowing it was driving her friend crazy. Then, instead of answering, she hung up the phone.

Steve Perry started blaring again, and she enjoyed his voice while gazing out at the desert horizon. The stunning morning view over the Arizona desert remained. And so did her soaring bird. Was it the same one?

*Mountains? Biking? Is she joking? Lu never rides bikes. She gets into these flings. Benji? I mean, she practically just met him.*

Her phone buzzed in her pants pocket. Amanda checked it. It read: "I need to know NOW. I know that wasn't the reception, bitch."

*You'll have to leave Santa Monica eventually, Mandi…*

A gust of wind was strong enough to push away any more thoughts. And it was so strong that it forced her to veer toward the opposite side of the highway. She felt terror rise in her chest as she struggled with the steering wheel, swerving the car back and forth, trying to merge back into her lane. Her VW Bug shook like crazy. Then her tires screeched as she slammed on her brakes. Her body was thrown back as her car stopped right before an incoming freeway barrier. Her hood missed a metal bar by inches. Or had she hit it? She wasn't sure. She looked down the road ahead, expecting to see a semi or something else huge that had pushed her. All she could make out was a black streak in the distance. A reflection? A mirage? It didn't look like a car, and it vanished after a few more seconds.

Then a larger streak of black flashed by her, shaking the car. She could make out this object more clearly. It looked like a dark orb racing at incredible speed into the distant horizon.

She unlatched her seat belt, threw her door open, and leaped out of her car. Then she placed her hand over her forehead, gazing down the freeway. There was nothing around for miles. She was completely alone out here. It was quiet, too quiet, as if nothing had happened.

She checked her car. There wasn't a scratch.

She took a deep breath and gazed at the view again. In the distance was that same gorgeous desert sunrise; vast saguaros, for as far as the eye could see, shone under golden light. She tried to calm herself by staring at the gorgeous view, but her hands still shook. Then she spotted that bird again. An eagle? A hawk? It was a huge bird soaring by the dunes and cacti as if watching her.

She turned at the sound of an approaching car. That was weird. There hadn't been anyone for miles a second ago. And when she had a better look at the car, that was a surprise too. It was a slick sports car, black as hell, with the windows completely tinted. The luxurious car pulled right behind her green VW.

The door opened and the first thing to come out were dusty black boots. This was followed by a tall man in black jeans and a black T-shirt. His dark hair was short, almost like a crew cut. He wasn't clean shaven, but his stubble was attractive. He was tanned, but his skin looked whiter with all the black clothes he wore. And he wore super dark opaque shades. In those sunglasses he reminded her of a cop.

"Are you all right, miss?" he asked. And he said that just like an officer too.

At first, he was expressionless behind his shades. But then, as Amanda turned to face him, he weirdly stepped back.

"I'm fine," Amanda said. "Fine." She took a deep

breath and threw back her long blond hair. "Just shaken up, I guess. Some truck almost threw me off the road, I think."

He looked down at her chest. She followed his eyes and saw what had shocked him. Her white T-shirt was splashed with red. She reached up and touched her dripping nose. "Shit." She wiped blood from the back of her hand. Then she reached into her pants pocket for a tissue, but it was empty.

"I saw you lose control of your car," the stranger said, walking closer.

"Where'd you come from?" She laughed. Then she smeared more blood from her face on the back of her hand. "Did you see the truck that pushed me?"

"Your nose is bleeding. Here." He reached into a pocket for some tissue, dipping down his head and peering over his shades. *Holy shit!* His eyes were the most gorgeous blue Amanda had ever seen. What a crime to cover them! He handed her the tissue, closing her hand over it. And she almost died. Right then and there, it was almost all over. With her fatigue and near accident, and those eyes peering over his shades, she felt unsteady.

*Get a hold of yourself, idiot!*

"Are you okay?" he asked.

"Fine. Fine. I'm fine." She pushed away from him and laughed nervously. "Not used to driving this early in the morning, I suppose. And … shook up, I guess."

"Well, I get it. You gave me quite a scare, miss. We're not far from Yuma. If you want, I can escort you to the border."

"Huh? Oh … it's just a nosebleed. I'm fine." She nervously chuckled. Then she wiped her nose again with his tissue. She smiled at him. "Just looks terrible with all the blood. You some kind of cop, or something?"

His face went deadpan, just like it had when she had first seen him. He didn't respond. He just stared at her.

Then he finally said, "That idiot on a bike almost hit you. I saw you swerve to avoid him. Guy was probably drunk."

"Oh."

*Wait? Bike? How could a motorcycle have pushed my car!*

He stood for a moment in silence just looking at her. It was like he was scrutinizing her, from her feet up to her face. He shook his head. "Well, have a nice day, ma'am. I'm glad you're safe."

And he headed back to his car.

She quickly blurted out, "Wait. Hey, what sort of car is that?"

He opened the door. Then he looked up and paused for a moment. "A client's. I'm delivering it from LA."

"Oh. I'm from LA."

"I figured that from your direction. Be careful out there, okay, Amanda?"

"Sure. Bye."

"Goodbye."

She held his handkerchief to her nose as she heard the roar of his engine. Then he drifted aggressively across the red desert sand, heading back onto the highway. She waved, watching him until she couldn't see his car anymore. Then she was alone on the desert highway again.

When she got back into her car, she put her hands on the steering wheel and tried to get a hold of herself. Her body was still shaking. She looked at her window and noticed blood on the beige cloth of her car door. "Shit." Then she looked at the passenger side. The cactus pot was broken on the floor. "Double shit."

Then she gasped. He had said "Amanda." "Amanda."

*How did he know my name!*

# 3

## THE HERO

THE SOUND OF CLICKS AND BELLS AMID THE SMELL OF smoke filled the large hall as John walked down a wide, red-carpeted walkway. It was early afternoon on a Saturday, but that didn't stop the casino from being loud. People were shouting by the craps tables beside the beeps, fake coin collections, and lever pulls. John wore his black leather jacket. Having been to Las Vegas enough times, he knew they loved overdoing the air conditioning in the casinos. It might be ninety outside, but it was usually sixty inside. And it was. He kept his shades on too. He didn't care to talk to anyone. He brooded. He couldn't stop thinking about the last mark. That last angel down looked so familiar. Too familiar. The whole meeting near Yuma was so weird.

*Sherry? Could it be?*

He thought of visiting Sherry's place and telling her about it. He considered it…but then thought better. He hadn't rested in days.

He was nearly done traversing the walkway toward the elevators. His thoughts of Amanda and Sherry left him as he passed a roulette table.

Sitting by the wheel was a captivating redhead, one of

the most beautiful women he had ever seen. She sat perched on a stool wearing a sparkly white dress and a matching diamond purse. The sleeves elegantly flowed over her wrists, touching the backs of her hands. Her hair was long, soft, and strikingly dark red. She pushed it from her eyes as she looked around. But when she saw him walking toward the table, she quickly looked away. Yet he caught a glimpse of a smile as her dainty fingers glided over her bangs.

He wasn't the only one staring. Across from her was a group of sharply dressed kids, very young, talking way too loud and casting stray glances at her.

John sat on an empty seat right beside the redhead. Then he waited for the wheel to stop spinning. He reached into his jeans pocket and pulled out a hundred-dollar bill. He laid it on the table. The redhead faced him and smiled a beautiful smile with perfect white teeth. A dealer wearing a formal black pin-striped suit handed him four chips.

"Red," he said, placing all the chips on red. The redhead put a chip on black.

"Come on, man!" exclaimed one of the young idiots across from him. "Let's go! Let's make some money."

When the dealer finally turned to face John, she had way too big a grimace. It was Lilith. Lilith. The same Lilith riding the motorcycle he had chased near Yuma, who had nearly taken Amanda's life. But now Lilith was disguised. The devil wore a dark wig covering her white hair and contacts that made her eyes black. Lilith's natural eyes were pink. But she couldn't darken her pale white skin. And the wig was too curly to be attractive. Still, her facial features were pretty. Lilith had always been a pretty demon.

"Azrael," Lilith said, smirking at John. "Azrael, welcome to Sin City. How surprising to see you here."

She glared at him with those fake eyes and seemed to relish his recognition. From the corner of his eye, John caught the redhead biting her lip, and her hand holding her chips was shaking. The other guys, facing her, tapped their fingers impatiently on the green cloth table.

"Place your bets," Lilith said, finally breaking eye contact with him. "Place your bets."

Lilith moved her pale hand over the table. She threw a small white ball on the wheel. The ball rolled around and around. John looked over his shades as Lilith turned back, folding her arms and glaring at him, waiting for the ball to land. The ball hit black. Lilith frowned at John and smugly collected his chips.

"You know you can win a lot more by choosing a number," said a boy with greased-back hair across the table.

"Fuck off," John said, glowering at Lilith.

"What!" the boy said, jumping up, raising a fist. "What the hell did you say!"

"I'm talking to her," John said, nodding at Lilith.

Lilith smirked.

"Hey," said the redheaded stranger. John had almost forgotten about her. "That was a lot of money you lost, mister. I'm sorry."

"No problem," John said, gladly turning away from Lilith to the redhead. "But I see you won."

She nodded and smiled. The dealer handed her another red chip.

"What's your name?" John asked her.

"Her name is Bridgette," Lilith said.

"I was asking her."

"And I answered for her."

"Come on, let's go," said the kids across from John. One of the guys was still staring at John, but his buddy tugged at him. They left the gambling table. That left Bridgette and John alone with the devil.

"I was told to meet you," Bridgette said quietly. She

waved her red hair back from her eyes. "Your name is John, right?"

"I think so."

"John, Bridgette," said Lilith, gesturing to them. "Bridgette, John. I hope she meets your expectations during this sanctuary, Azrael? She matches your taste. Does she not? She's quite lovely, isn't she?"

"I wasn't aware we were in sanctuary," John said. "It seems sanctuary is whatever the hell you and Samael call it. But she is pretty. Yes. Very."

"Always the best for Raphael's agents." Lilith turned to the rest of the table, but there was no one there. "Place your bets. Place your bets."

John reached into his wallet and took out ten more hundred-dollar bills.

"You think it'll be red this time?" John turned and leaned toward Bridgette. "I tell you what, if I win, I'll give you some of my winnings."

"I hope you win for your sake," she said, widening her large eyes. "That's a lot of money, mister. Good luck."

She had lovely eyes and perfect white teeth. An angelic smile.

"We've decided to kill Amanda tomorrow," Lilith said as the metal ball spun. "Unusual? Perhaps. But this mark is unusual, isn't she? Did you recognize her? I'd think you would. We made sure that this mark particularly interested you. Well, you might have won yesterday, but we've decided on another go on the road. What do you think?"

Bridgette put her hand on John's. He turned, surprised. Bridgette smiled uncomfortably. Her hand flapped a bit over his. She was doing a job, obviously.

"Go on," John said, looking at Bridgette. "What's the deal?"

"I shall tell you after you lose," Lilith said with a chuckle. "I shall tell you after you get used to losing. Life is like a bet, you know, and you have repeatedly picked the wrong side."

The white ball hit black.

"See?"

"It's all right." John pulled another hundred dollars out of his wallet and handed the cash to Bridgette.

"You said if you won?" Bridgette said, furrowing her brow.

"Who said I lost? When are we meeting?"

"Huh?" Bridgette asked, flustered. "Oh." Her face flushed almost as red as her hair.

"That's why Lilith introduced us, right?" John asked.

"Oh… I don't know. When?"

"Midnight," he said. "I'll see you then." He handed her his key card envelope with his room number and the spare key card. Bridgette nodded and tucked it in her purse. "Now, excuse us, but I need to have a word with your procurer."

John watched Bridgette leave. He couldn't help but stare at her legs under her sparkly dress. Lilith had done her job, indeed. She was perfect.

"Go on," John said, turning back.

"Life is a game of chance, is it not?" Lilith said, folding her arms over her suit. Then she showed her empty palms as if she were a magician. "Red or black? You never know. Is your allegiance to Michael? Gabriel? Raphael? Samael? Or… God?" She laughed. "Where does your soul lie?" She leaned forward. "Here's why we're meeting. From now on, I propose you and I converge in public in Las Vegas. I approach angels on the verge of ascension, you fuck them, and save their miserable lives by defiling them. They can then wait for perdition, like you. It will be as useful as your meddling with me on the road. Then we can stop the tiresome chase. It'll all be discreet and private, far more relaxing and satisfying for both you and me. You know we can't keep fighting in public like this. Eventually someone's going to be found. So how does that sound? Instead of the road?" And the bitch finished with a big smirk.

"Fuck you."

"You are Bridgette's guardian angel tonight," Lilith said with a laugh. "She's my gift. But I've marked her too. So you work for me tonight. If you don't guard her, I kill her. If you screw her, I *might* kill her… I *might* not. You never know. Place your bets. And then, after we've had our fun, tomorrow we meet for the real game. On the highway. For Amanda. Or…" She looked at him with disgustingly fake pity in her fake eyes. "*Was she Sherry?*"

John placed a hundred on the table. "Red."

"I'd say you're a masochist."

"I have a feeling the table's rigged. I want to prove it. Odds are I'll win on a third try."

"Odds are you will always lose without me." Lilith stroked his hand with her pale fingers. He jerked away. "Instead of the redhead tonight, you know, you…and I could be together? What do you think? After all, carnal pleasure can lead to the heart. Perhaps a taste of me will lead you finally along the right path. What do you say?"

"I'd rather be with the girl. She's prettier." He pushed the bill toward her again. "Red."

Lilith hissed at him. She grabbed his hundred-dollar bill and pushed a black chip on red. Then she hurled the white ball in the air. It landed perfectly on the spinning wheel.

"Red or black," she snapped. "Hmm, Azrael? What shall you be? Life is simply a game of chance. Nothing more, nothing less. You've been working for the wrong side. I offer pleasure, Raphael offers pain. When will you get this?" The ball landed on green. "Ah. See. Neither wins. But you still lose." The bitch laughed. "Perhaps this is the real Azrael. Destined to be green. A *John*? A drifter roaming roads saving people from peace and happiness? Work for me and all pain ends. All Samael and I offer you is pleasure. I shall demonstrate tonight."

"I save lives."

"I retire souls to heaven," Lilith said with a shrug. "Enjoy your prize. You deserve it for thwarting the death of the young Sherry yesterday. But tomorrow morning ends our sanctuary. We fight again on the road."

~

Bridgette stirred in bed. When she got up and stretched her arms, her breasts and perfect figure were silhouetted by the light emitted from the window. She yawned. Then he stared at her naked ass under her long red hair as she swayed to the floor-to-ceiling window. She pressed a button opening the drapes, and the lights of the city that never sleeps were unveiled before them. Now her knock-out nude body shone in the light.

"So pretty," she said with a yawn. "I love these rooms. Always working, I forget how breathtaking it is for the guests. You on vacation, hero?"

"Don't call me a hero."

She ran her fingers along the drapes and gazed down at the city lights. Then she yawned again. Her face, her stunning face, was silhouetted by the glow from the Las Vegas Strip.

"You want something to drink?" John asked.

"What do you have?"

"Fuck if I know. There's a fridge under the cabinet. Take whatever you want."

"Thanks," she said with a laugh.

She meandered over and then bent down, waving her ass before him as she searched the small refrigerator. He was sure she was doing that on purpose. Then she grabbed two palm-sized bottles of alcohol and closed the door.

"You best not be a cop," she said, cocking her head back. "Are you? I know you don't work for my contact."

"How do you know that?"

She sat beside him on the bed. She handed him one bottle and then unscrewed the other and drank it. He laid his on the nearby nightstand.

"You were fighting with her." She shrugged. "You seemed to hate each other."

"I'm not a cop."

"Hmm." She turned her back to him. "You kinda act like one."

"I'm not a cop."

"Can you scratch my back?" She turned her back to him again.

He ran his fingers along her neck and down her back, massaging deep into the skin.

"Ohhh," she said, closing her eyes, "you have such nice strong hands."

He pressed deeper and she bent forward. He ran his fingers over her nipples and his palms traced the curves of her breasts. She leaned back, shaking her hair out. Then she moaned. "That's it. Perfect."

"What should we do now?" she whispered. "You asked in the note that I wear black. Why?"

"Black is my color."

"Maybe you should have picked black when you put your money down."

"I didn't say it was my favorite color. Your hair's red."

"You're weird, you know that?" she said, cocking her head back. Then she laughed and put a hand up. "No offense. I mean, you're just weird. So were your friends. They were really weird too." She closed her eyes and relaxed again as he dug further with his fingers. "That feels so good."

Bridgette had lived all her life in Las Vegas, she had told him. She had wanted to be a teacher. But she didn't have money for school. So she whored. It didn't start that way. It started in a strip club. Now she wanted out of Sin City, just like John wanted out of his job. She wasn't happy. Neither was John.

Of course Lilith had picked the girl simply as a tease, a mockery of his job. A trap. Did he accept pleasure in pain? Either way, the damage was already done, and the prostitute's fate was inevitable. Like Amanda, this girl was marked. She would die. Just like Amanda.

"That feels so good." She drank more from the small bottle of alcohol. "You're really weird." She swallowed and put a hand up again. "Not in a bad way. Just weird. You don't seem to fit in. Ohhh… That feels so good, hero, keep rubbing like that…"

She turned and kissed his lips. Then she ran her long fingernails along his groin and touched the bulge in his underwear. She probed inside and touched his hard cock. Then she rubbed it up and down with one hand, while massaging his chest and stomach with the other hand, still holding the mini–liquor bottle.

"Perhaps we've had enough," John said, pulling away.

But he smelled her again. Roses. He wondered if she had added the scent after leaving the roulette wheel. Lilith knew he loved that scent. She probably gave it to Bridgette. She must have. Bridgette rubbed along his leg as she sucked on his lip. Then she entered his mouth and ran her tongue along his.

He'd let her in the room when she'd opened it with his key. Sure. To protect her, he had told himself. And then he'd let her kiss him. Sure, he'd let her do that. To keep the pretense. But that was it. At first…

She giggled and turned to him, staring into his eyes. It was dark but lit enough by the window to see her lovely profile. And her stunning eyes, opened wider in the dim light. They both froze. He felt hypnotized gazing at her. Then she ran her hand along the stubble of his cheek and over his short hair. For a moment, just a moment, he thought of lying down beside her and drifting to sleep. Not lying with her, but just lying beside her. That was enough to *protect* her.

"You want me now, hero?"

"Don't call me a hero," he snapped, lifting a finger. "Don't do that."

She snatched his raised finger with a laugh. Then, slowly, she sucked it. Up and down, as if she were sucking his cock. Gently, she pushed him on his back. "Relax," she said. She sat on her knees, bare breasted with the light from the window shadowing her perfect figure. Then she bent down and whispered in his ear, "I want to suck your cock and taste it. Then I want you inside me, lover. I'll be on top. Please. Let's do that. I want you to fuck me again. Okay? How about we do that, John?"

He could just see Lilith glowering at him now, those spooky, unnatural pink eyes, knowing full well that he suffered in her entanglement. Protect her and sleep on the couch? Yeah, right. He wasn't a hero, and he wasn't innocent either.

She gently touched her lips to his again. Ever so slightly. She smelled so nice. Behind the alcohol was that flowery aroma. He couldn't quite place it: Was it roses? Carnations? It didn't smell slutty. He liked that.

She pulled back for a moment and tipped her small bottle of alcohol into her mouth, downing the rest. Then she giggled and scooted on her knees to the foot of the bed.

"You don't like the word *hero*, huh?" she asked, looking

up at him, pulling down his underwear to his ankles. "What should I call you then?"

"John."

"Is that really your name?"

"No."

"I didn't think so," she said with a laugh. "What's your real name?"

"Nothing."

"You want me to call you *Nothing*?"

He shrugged. She shook her head and pushed him flat on his back.

"You're not nothing, mister. Not with that cock."

And he lay still. And she sucked. He didn't move. She did. So everything was all right. *Right?* He leaned back, gazing up at the ceiling in darkness, trying to think of nothing. While she took his cock into her mouth and sucked him. Up and down. Up and down along his shaft.

Then she jumped up, surprising him. She straddled him.

"Sorry, Mr. Nothing, but I can't wait anymore," she said and laughed. "I want you inside me. Now."

She tore a condom packet open and rolled the condom on his dick—where she'd gotten it, he wasn't sure. Then she glided his cock inside her, bobbing up and down, running her hands along her breasts and then sucking his index finger while riding him.

She moaned as she gave him pleasure. Riding him. And this was it. This was his true sanctuary. He imagined Lilith's pink eyes staring into his, her mouth curled in a sinister, sardonic grin mocking his damned soul.

But he wouldn't give himself in to the pleasure. He wouldn't even move. Especially not now. He felt more miserable than ever. Of course Lilith had known he would. That's why she had arranged it.

Bridgette orgasmed, shaking over John's body. Then she fell to his side. He hadn't moved since she mounted him.

"Are you okay?" she asked, sounding confused. She ran her hand through his hair. "You're not done, baby."

"I'm fine," he said, turning his head from her.

"You're a nice guy," she said, nodding as if explaining it to herself. "Really nice. That's what you are. You're just a nice guy."

"I'm not a nice guy."

By morning her naked body lay sprawled on the white sheets of the bed. Her eyes were open, but glassy. She lay there on her back, in the spot where they'd had sex. He had stepped into the bathroom only for a moment. That had been enough time for them to break in quietly and suffocate her. But this would be easy for his enemies to cover up. Who'd care about a wandering prostitute?

She was dead. He had failed at protecting this wandering soul. To John, it didn't matter if they were pure or if they were prostitutes. A life was a life. Lilith knew that. The devil had won. She would either turn him or make him lose his mind.

On the other pillow one word was scratched on a note: *Colorado.*

# 4

## MESA VERDE

Amanda leaned over a wood fence staring at the square stone structures way off in the distance. She let out a big sigh. Because she loved it. She had learned that around the thirteenth century, ancestral Pueblo Native Americans built their homes deep in the recesses of the hillside. No one knows why. Maybe for shelter? Then they were all strangely abandoned. Gazing at them from this lookout from so far away hardly did them justice. But really, Amanda wasn't looking just at them. She loved the views beyond the horizon even more. Ever since Albuquerque, the endless horizons had taken her breath away. The infinite horizon was like the shore by the beach, only this wasn't water. This was different, something she never saw in LA.

A gentle breeze blew against her cheek. It blew along her short white skirt too. The weather was just perfect.

She turned to the gentleman closest to her amid the crowd. He had parched, wrinkled dark skin and a cowboy hat and was enjoying the view too.

"Excuse me," Amanda said to him. "Can you take a picture of me?"

She posed in front of the fence hoping she wouldn't block the ruins.

He smiled. Then he handed her back the phone.

*Happy enough. Check.*

She turned around and leaned on the rail, staring out and sighing again.

*Ancient pueblo village. Check.*

*Better move out now, Amanda, if you're gonna make it to Grand Junction before nightfall.*

Then she snapped her fingers. She had almost forgotten her podcast! She pulled out her handheld recorder from her pants pocket.

"Guys, I'm here in front of Mesa Verde. Have you ever been? It's so incredible. There's this crack in the Earth and inside, pretty far away— it isn't a bear in a bear cave. No. No. It's an actual ancient city. I'm not kidding. A whole Pueblo town. They call it Step House. And they say it's a thousand years old. From here, it's kinda small. Like I can imagine a bear coming out and the houses just being rocks. But there's all these open square windows over the rocks too. So… I'm talking softly because a bunch of tourists are standing real close looking at the village but throwing a couple stray glances at me like I'm a total psycho. But I had to tell you about it live right now 'cause I'm right here right now, guys. If you're ever in West Colorado, you've got to check this out. You just got to."

She clicked the off button with a satisfied nod.

That's when she noticed a tall boy with a black T-shirt and jeans to her left. He was super pale and wearing shades. The boy was close enough to hear her recording. That must have been the source of his big grin.

"I have these if you want to try," he said, offering her binoculars.

He had a friend who was also wearing shades and really pale, but heavier. Behind the sunglasses, they had pink eyes.

"Thanks," Amanda said.

With the binoculars she could make out the individual holes in each square building. She saw stone steps and holes for firepits in the sand. And she saw people hiking around the ruins that she hadn't spotted with her naked eye.

"Have you checked out the petroglyphs?" the tall, pale guy asked.

"No," she said, not tearing her eyes from the view.

"We're backpacking tomorrow. I'm Charlie. We're hiking the whole area."

"My name's Amanda." But she was still looking through the binoculars. She spotted a couple climbing up steps into one of the rooms. And another, a bit ahead of them, walking through a crack in a stone wall.

"We just came back. We can go there again with you, Amanda, if you want to check it out?"

"It's too far," Amanda said, finally handing him back the binoculars. "I don't have time."

"The walk to the Step House is less than an hour."

"What brings you here?" asked Charlie's friend.

"Graduation present."

"Oh, are you with your parents?"

"No."

"Friends?"

She smiled and shook her head.

"So you're alone?" asked Charlie.

"Yeah. A gift to myself."

Charlie smiled again, but with a squint that meant he thought she seemed a little weird. He glanced at his friend.

"Well, bye," Amanda said, waving her hand. "And thanks. I gotta get going. It's gonna get dark and I've got a long drive." Honestly, they were creeping her out.

"Where're you heading?"

"Cross country."

"Where?" asked Charlie.

"Across the country."

That was enough. She wasn't going to tell these creepy guys another thing. And, anyway, she had to leave. She had spent too much time already trying to find Mesa Verde. Her hotel reservations were on the outskirts of Grand Junction, and she had a long drive yet.

She made her way back to the parking lot to her green VW Bug. But as she walked along the dirt walkway, she caught the two strangers trailing behind her. At first, she thought nothing of it because Charlie was nonchalantly drinking water from a straw in his backpack, gazing back at the cliffs, while the other guy just stared ahead with his hands in his pockets. But then, by a fork in the road heading to her car, they came right behind her.

But they turned the opposite direction in the parking lot and got in a beat-up white pickup truck. Thankfully, they just sat in their truck as she left the park.

She turned on the radio. It was the Eagles—the last song on her *Hotel California* album. A bit too mellow, so she switched the tune to her all-time favorite song on the album, "Try and Love Again."

Back on the road, it was just an empty desert—which she loved. She tapped her hand on the steering wheel to the music. But the song was interrupted by her phone ringing.

"Hey, babe!"

"What's up, Lu?"

"Finally got you. I texted you to call hours ago."

"God, you're like my mom. She hasn't even called yet." Amanda leaned forward and gazed between the trees as the horizon opened up again. The view seemed to go on forever. "Lu, I wish you could see what I see. The view is to die for."

"Take some pics and send them to me."

"It's not the same."

"Where's your next stop?"

"Denver. I was thinking of changing course to Mount Rushmore. But it's just so far, but my listeners would have loved it. Now I can check off Mesa Verde. Did you know Mesa Verde was the first national park in the US? It was so great."

"I really don't give a shit. Sorry, Mands."

Amanda laughed. "It's something you gotta see if you're driving across country."

"Well, I never heard of it."

"'Cause you've never traveled across country."

"Okay. But, ya know, I have been to the mountains. Speaking of such, have you decided?"

Amanda stopped listening to her. Not because she wanted to play mean again, but because she caught sight of a white pickup truck behind her. It was about a half mile back, but it seemed to be following her. And it was definitely the same truck those two strange boys got into when she was in the parking lot. Were they heading to Grand Junction too? Had they left the parking lot at exactly the same time she had? Maybe. But didn't they tell her they were backpacking at the park tomorrow?

"Well?" asked Lu through her car speakers. "What do you say? How about it?"

"Huh?"

"What's the matter, Mandi?"

"Oh…nothing. I'm just wondering why these guys are following me."

"What! Amanda, I told you that you shouldn't be driving alone."

"Yeah. Well—" There were a few cars between them, but they were there. "They're two guys I met at the Pueblo village ruins. They didn't really seem dangerous, just nerdy."

"Sometimes the greatest serial killers are nerdy."

"Thanks a lot, Lu. You're making me feel a whole lot better."

Now they were at least a half mile behind her. She watched as they disappeared for a moment behind a hillside. Then they appeared again around a bend.

"You just came from a national park?" asked Luane. "Why not just turn around and talk to a park ranger?"

"I'm fine. There's only one highway out here."

"Well, you're scaring the shit out of me. Just pull over and see if they pass."

"I want to get to Grand Junction before it gets dark." But Luane's idea was, in fact, perfect.

Amanda pulled over.

"Gone?" Luane asked after a moment.

They drove by her car.

"Yeah." Amanda took a deep breath.

"Stop freaking me out!" Luane said with a sigh. "Shit. Call the minute you reach Grand Junction, okay?"

"Sure."

"And don't go to Mount Rushmore. Just do your cross-country thing, stay at Grand Junction, and then get your ass back home."

"But what about my fans?"

"Stop it, Mands."

"Okay," Amanda said with a laugh. "Bye, Lu."

"Wait, hey, what about—"

Amanda chuckled as she wickedly hung up the phone. She honestly didn't know yet where she wanted to spend her summer. If she lost the cabin, she lost the cabin.

She watched the white pickup travel past some trees up ahead and then disappear around another corner.

Now she only hoped that she'd arrive at her hotel before nightfall. It was getting late.

**5**

—————

# SHATTERED GLASS

There was no way Amanda was making it to Grand Junction before nightfall. It was already dark. Really dark. She had her brights on, but she saw so many shadows under the moon. That made her imagination race in fantasy. Because there were no other cars on the road. She was on a deserted highway with nothing out here, not even any radio reception. She kept playing old classic rock music, now listening to the band Asia, but her favorite oldies didn't stop her from feeling uneasy. Especially when a car's headlights started trailing her along the deserted highway, winding up a hill.

She estimated she had only another hour or so of driving, but she wasn't sure. The last sign had said Grand Junction in eighty-eight miles. Even at seventy-five miles an hour, that had been over half an hour ago.

She jumped as the car behind her turned. Under the moonlight, she saw a white pickup truck.

*What! How?*

She had lost them a hundred miles ago. It couldn't be the same car. Could it?

But then the vehicle came closer, swerving in and out of its lane. It didn't pass, it came right up alongside her car, close enough for Amanda to recognize the beat-up pickup truck. She touched the console and typed in Luane's number on speed dial. Nothing. There was no reception.

*What's Luane gonna do for you anyway?*

The passenger window rolled down and she recognized the guys from Mesa Verde. Yes, it was their same pale features visible by the dim lights of the truck cabin. And most weirdly, they were wearing shades. One of them was drinking from a bottle, the one Amanda recognized as Charlie. He was driving. They gestured for her to roll down her window.

She shook her head.

"Amanda, your back tire's flat."

"What?" Amanda asked, cupping her ear.

They both signaled for her to roll down the window again. Amanda shook her head.

"Your back tire," Charlie hollered, pointing to the back of her car. "It's flat. We can help."

"Forget it," Amanda shouted. She gestured with her hand for them to shoo. "Go away."

Charlie cupped his ear. They moved their pickup so close to her car that she swerved to avoid hitting them. Then she caught them laughing inside their car.

She sped up ahead, climbing a short incline. When she reached the top, she caught a flash of light behind trailing her from the valley below. At first, she figured it was a plane. It was traveling at a speed not possible for any car. But then she noticed it followed the turns of the road. Under moonlight, she recognized it in the far distance as a sleek black car; the same car she had seen near Yuma. Her stranger! Here? Hundreds of miles away? How? But somehow, he *was* here, and that made her less tense. But then the black car cut its headlights and disappeared.

She heard more drunken laughter. The truck was paralleling her again, this time on her right side.

"Hey, Amanda," Charlie cried, laughing. "Here! Maybe this will help."

*Crash!*

Glass fell all over her lap. She quickly brushed it off as if it was poison. Then she screamed. She grabbed the wheel as her car swerved out of the lane. She must have accidentally moved the steering wheel during the explosion. She gripped the wheel tight, bracing for another attack.

There was a crash, this one much louder, but it didn't come from her car. Wheels squealed. There was another bang. Looking behind through her rearview mirror the headlights of the pickup truck flickered and spun in darkness, blinking out beside the road. Had it rolled off the highway?

Lying on the passenger seat among all the pieces of broken glass was the source of her terror: a large stone the size of a brick.

Amanda pressed the gas pedal to the floor. The whoosh of wind and the sound of her car through her now open window were the only sounds she heard as she barreled down the empty highway. She brought her VW up to over one hundred and ten. Her foot was all the way down on the floor. It even hurt pressing down so hard. But all she cared about now was getting the hell out of here.

Her hand shook. She glanced through all her mirrors. She was alone. Alone again on this dark, empty highway.

She drove in solitude in complete darkness for another mile without looking back. Only forward. Her only goal was to get to Grand Junction. If her window had still been intact, she could have thought her terror had all been imagined. But there was still a rush of wind and road noise over her right shoulder.

Amanda didn't slow down. And in her excitement, she

nearly crashed, losing control of the car on a sharp turn. The road straightened and she pressed as hard on the gas pedal as she could.

She jumped at the roar of an engine beside her. Headlights switched on the right shoulder of the highway. The truck? Were they back?! Amanda turned sharply, almost being thrown off the highway. But she discerned her stranger again driving right beside her, paralleling her car.

"Pull over," someone shouted.

In the darkness, Amanda made out a man, behind dim, multicolored lights, inside the car. He had opened his window. She recognized his voice. It was definitely her stranger from the desert near Yuma. The oddest thing was that the man was wearing, like those goons, shades at night.

"Pull over," the man said again. "You're driving too fast, Amanda."

"I won't," she shouted back into the wind. "I can't trust strangers."

"We've already met. Pull over."

"I already met them too!"

"I took care of them."

*Took care of them? What the hell does that mean?*

All she could see behind her was darkness. Then she turned back to her stranger. She quickly shook her head.

"All right," he said. "But slow down. You're driving too fast."

"I can take care of myself. I have mace." And that was an absolutely ridiculous thing to say.

"I'll go," he shouted back. "Just slow down for your safety. Please."

He sped ahead of her, pulled in front, and zoomed past, becoming a blur. The light disappeared over the horizon. It was so weird. She felt like she had witnessed a UFO.

Then all became quiet again as if nothing had

happened. Only the sound of the wind blowing hard through her shattered window.

He said they were taken care of. What did her dark stranger do? *Kill them?*

She wouldn't tell anyone. She wouldn't tell Lu or her parents—God, she could never tell her parents. Her mom had insisted she not go alone on this trip. She'd cover the window in plastic and not tell a soul about the vandalism. Maybe she'd say a stone fell from a cliff or something. Nor would she tell a soul about her UFO.

Perhaps she was going mad? Perhaps it was all a dream created by driving in desolation on the dark deserted highway?

*Your window was smashed by drunken idiots, Mands. Is that rush of air in the car a dream?*

*No, more like a nightmare.*

The rest of her drive back to civilization was one of the most torturous drives she had ever had in her life.

Amanda got up when it was still dark, early in the morning, and wheeled her luggage back to the parking lot. On the far-off horizon, there was a red shine. The sun was rising. She was still tired. She hadn't slept all night. But she wanted to move on.

When she approached her car, she gasped. Her car had been washed. The broken window was repaired. She was so surprised that she touched the glass, thinking perhaps she was going crazy. But there it was. The glass was cold, but spotless. The inside of her car was clean too. The stone that had broken the window was gone, and, along with it, all the remnants of fast food, sauce packs and empty soda cups, leftover clothing bags, socks and hats, everything was neatly arranged over a freshly vacuumed interior. Her car had never been this clean. There was a note under her windshield wiper. She unfolded and read it:

*Fly home. Avoid the roads. They're hunting you on the highway.*

**6**

---

## ANGEL DIVE

"I'M SORRY, JOHN."

John was back at a bar in a secluded café in the middle of the night. And Sherry was doing her usual thing, standing across the bar, fighting his wishes for more and more whiskey. It seemed they had been doing the same thing for years. And he cherished it. She smiled a rueful grin, gathering up the wrinkles on her face. Her long silvery hair flowed over her T-shirt and jeans. Old? Sure she was, but she was beautiful.

Angel Dive was an old-fashioned desert café, a dump really, but Sherry's dump. The most welcoming place in the world. The burgundy walls of the restaurant held the usual decorative bar things: a dart board, a pool table, and a stage for entertainment. In the corner, facing the lone parking lot, windows looked out on the desert. But the café was in the middle of nowhere, miles from any other establishment. Sherry seemed to like that. And she liked talking to drifters, like John. On Fridays, it'd be busy. Not tonight. Not now. Tonight there was only a couple at the opposite side of the place sitting at a wooden table.

"I'm sorry, John," Sherry said again with a rueful grin.

She cleaned the counter around him with a towel. Then she peered deep into his eyes. She had lovely large eyes. The exact same eyes as Amanda. "Rick said you were almost done. Why are they torturing you like this? Why is it so hard for it all to be over?"

"It's always hard," he said, downing another glass of whiskey and slamming it on the corner. "There's always some test. It's never over."

"There shouldn't be. You're a good man."

"I'm not a good man," he said with a chuckle. "I'm not a good man at all. You know that."

"You're a good man, John."

"Do you know the last girl I fucked?"

"Not now," Sherry said, losing her smile. Then she looked around at the other customers. "The drinking's getting to your head."

He nodded and raised his finger. "Let me tell you about it."

Sherry leaned against a counter full of bottles and shook out her long gray hair in a huff. She folded her arms and rolled her eyes.

"I'll keep out the details of the sex," he said.

"Please."

"Lilith got me a hooker in Vegas."

"Jesus, John." Sherry rolled her eyes again. "And you took her?"

"It was a job," he said with a laugh. "Yeah, sort of." He tapped his glass. Sherry shook her head. John shook his head and tapped the glass harder. Sherry reached over for the bottle.

"You know what she called me, Sher?"

"Who?"

"The girl I fucked?"

"What? What did the whore call you? Like I care. I'm guessing, asshole?"

"She called me a hero."

"You are a hero, John."

"I'm not a fucking hero," he shouted, slamming the counter with his open palm.

The couple at the table looked over. Sherry, who rarely got angry over anything, looked pissed. "I warn you. I'll throw you out of my place if you go crazy here again. This is your last drink. Don't be acting like that around here."

"Our place," he said more quietly, staring at his glass. "It's our place, Sher. I'm not a hero."

"You are to me. You save lives. You're an angel, John. And you're my angel. You're a hero in my eyes. You always were, even before. You said you saved this Amanda. Why didn't it end? Why did they go back and hunt Amanda again?"

"They'll get her eventually. She's marked."

"I know. But the job's done. They always move on. Why'd they go back and attack her again? What did Rick say? If you save this last soul, will you ascend? Is this the last test? Is that why it's so hard? Please tell me." She shook her head and took a deep breath. "God, I don't want you to go, but I can't stand you like this. You're only getting worse."

"Does it matter?"

"Yeah, it could take your mind. Live or die, soul or eternal, you could lose a grasp of who you are."

"They already did that to me." Then he glared at her and pointed a finger. "You won't tell me my name."

"Shit, you're in such a mood tonight."

He stared at her. Her wrinkled face. He tried to place her. He tried to see if he could remember more than just his occasional memories. He searched her eyes. Her face. There was nothing right now. But he would see her young features again soon enough. It was just a matter of time before he was tortured once more. Was it torture? He liked being with her. He liked visions of her younger self. There was that in this hell of a world. Perhaps that was enough?

"I know you're hurting, John," Sherry said. "They're bringing it all back to you. But that doesn't mean you have to hurt me."

He was surprised to see a tear roll down her cheek. He reached for it.

"I've accepted our fate," Sherry said, shaking her head and swatting his hand. "You haven't. You're miserable because you won't accept the will of God."

"Oh come on, what is the will of God, Sher? Huh?" he asked, reaching over to touch her tear again on her wrinkled skin. She turned from him. "And what is this?"

"I'm crying for you, you jerk."

"Don't cry for me. I don't deserve it."

"I'll shed tears for you whenever I want. I still care about you."

"And I care about you," he said with a sigh. "I love you." He took her hand and ran his fingers along it. The wrinkles in her hands—he didn't care. He loved her hands. He loved her smile. He loved everything about her.

"I love you," John muttered. "Why do you think I'm here tonight?"

"This young girl, Amanda," she said with a sigh. "Tell me, John. She really looks like me?"

"Exactly like you." He downed another glass. "She's your double."

# 7

## SANCTUARY

JOHN FELT THE RUMBLE OF HIS ENGINE AND THE SLOW DRIFT of his car, almost hypnotic, as he sped across the desert. Multicolored light rushed past the edges of his windshield, splashing like colored raindrops and sparks. A mountain rose on the horizon. It left him behind as fast as it had appeared. Every inch his steering wheel turned was a sharp turn. He tracked the road following the lines lit by his headlights, cars passing over the deserted highway every few seconds, though they were miles apart. When he had first driven the car years ago, he had gripped the wheel tightly with the realization that an impact with anyone on the highway at this speed would be fatal—not for him but for anyone he collided with. Now, seasoned and worn, having wandered for years, he passed cars as if they were hills and valleys.

He pressed harder on the gas. The hills and horizon bent before his eyes. At this speed, every mile was a turn. This fast, the car itself aided him in impossible turns beyond his senses. He'd be invisible to the human eye now, visible only to, perhaps, spirits and specters of the dead stuck in this cesspool of a world, like him.

He felt desolation. Blessed loneliness. So he headed for his sanctuary.

Less than ten minutes from Arizona, he found himself in another desert. In Denver the temperature had been in the eighties during the day. Here in the Mojave Desert in the middle of the night, it was a nice seventy outside.

He slowed down as he approached his favorite spot. The drops of light stopped bouncing off the glass. The colors faded. Then he was in darkness in a canyon. But even if the sun were out, it'd be completely barren.

He turned on a dirt road only he knew about. In another moment, he was there.

Before him was a vast field of sand and salt. He shut off his headlights, and it was pitch black except the bright stars above. He got out of the car, and his black boots crackled along dry, caked dirt. Then he put his hands in his pockets and walked away from his car.

That's when the images came. Usually he turned from them. Not after seeing Amanda. The images always came to him more clearly when he was in the dark. He never slept because of them. Now he longed for them while awake. Now he could sift through them to try to make sense of the new mark. Amanda. To see if she really was who he thought she was. Perhaps he had only imagined the resemblance?

In a short time, a picture came to his mind as vivid as the stars.

He was on the beach in Southern California. It was afternoon. But just as now, he had his thumbs in the pockets of his jeans, was wearing shades, and was staring out at the sea.

"Where've you been?" asked a woman. Her voice was rough like Sherry's. It was exactly like Sherry's. It was her voice.

In his past images, he might have called her Sherry. But

this woman, with her long, flowing blond hair, smooth skin, and bright energy, didn't look like Sherry. She looked like the recent mark he had saved. Amanda. Her blond hair was covered by a wide-brimmed white beach hat, and she was wearing a beach throw with a red bathing suit. Her body was perfect, her face beautiful under large sunglasses.

They were standing on a cliffside. He could smell the salt and hear the waves.

She wasn't angry when she asked him that. She seemed happier than ever to just be beside him. She smiled sweetly.

"Away," he answered. "I've been away." He turned back to the view of the shore and leaned on the railing. "On business. But I'm happy to be back now."

"Well, I'm sure happy to see you," she said, rubbing his back. There was a bark and she looked down and laughed. She kneeled down and ran her hand over the hide of a large dog. "Bear's happy to see you too. Aren't you, boy? Huh, Bear?"

*Bear?*

The dog jumped on John's leg and barked. John just looked down. He didn't recall having a dog.

"Don't get on grumpy's leg now," Amanda said. "He doesn't like it. Jeeze, you could pet him, at least. You haven't seen us in weeks."

John kneeled down and ran his hand over the dog's head and under his neck. Bear barked and seemed to love it. John couldn't place this memory. He didn't recall having a dog.

John stood up straight again, looking out at the sea.

"How long will you be off next?" she asked.

"I don't know. I just got back."

"What happened?" she asked, sounding grave. "Tell me. Tell me something."

She had always been there for him. His sanctuary. He remembered that now. Even back then. Perhaps that's why

Sherry chose to work in a bar after he left. Surely she did the same for her patrons in Yuma. And she was his confidant. His listener.

He turned and saw the outline of a canyon. He remembered that he was still in Death Valley and that this vision wasn't real. But he liked this memory. He didn't want to be in the desert. He wanted to be back on the beach reliving this moment again.

"I can't tell you the details," John said, now talking to the valley walls. "It's just hard. The things I saw were—"

"It's gotta stop," Amanda said, shaking her head. She turned grave. "It's like you're a soldier, not a cop. And it's getting to your head. You should stop all this now."

He nodded. It was almost the same words Sherry had just told him in her restaurant. He turned to her and tipped his shades down. She shimmered. Although transparent, the outline of her white dress was yellow like the rays of the sun. But behind her, he could still see the dark desert canyon. "I have you."

"Aha." She took off her shades and kissed his lips. "There's me. You have me."

A slight ray of light was coming off the horizon. It was in the direction of his mirage of Amanda. It spread a violet tinge over the whole desert valley. The light awoke him from his dream, shining through the vision—this was the brightest light in this world. The sun.

But he still felt her. She leaned into him and tried to kiss him. His sunglasses hit her face. She laughed as she pulled back. "Why do you always wear these things?"

He shrugged.

"Well, now's as good a time as any," she said. "Time for some bad news. Tommy's in jail again."

"When is he ever not?" John asked with a laugh.

"He idolizes you. You're his brother."

"Cousin. He's an idiot. Tommy will always be an idiot."

"You know, when he's out, he's gonna end up dead."

"I don't think so. Why's he in jail this time?"

"You know he's got bad friends. It was the coke. He got involved with the wrong people and was framed. Can you spring him?"

"I'll see what I can do."

The vision faded. Amanda was gone.

John walked alone on the sand under the rising sun.

Then she appeared again, joyously laughing this time among grass and trees. And this time his young lover wore a white T-shirt and dark pants. But she had that same big white hat. Green trees and grass surrounded them. There was a towel on the grass where they had picnicked. And Bear was running around him, the dog he had forgotten. She was playing fetch with a squeeze toy.

John's phone rang.

"Yeah," John said in the darkness. The park faded. He was back in the desert valley.

"Angel down. Tori. She's nineteen, Black, with long hair. She goes to Boise State University. She's studying sociology. Born a Leo. She's going on a date downtown. That's their lead."

"Samael or Lilith?"

"Samael, we think. Lilith was last spotted closer to Nebraska. Where you at?"

"Not far from there."

"From what I hear from Michael, you're so close to earning your wings, man. Just hang in there. Don't let this last test tear you up."

"Why so young?"

"What?"

"You said nineteen. Why is the angel so young? They don't go after kids."

"Nineteen isn't a kid. And how the fuck should I know, John? Or give a shit? You gotten over being a budding journalist? The look-alike. It's not her. It's not Sherry. Can I trust you to be on the case, or are you going to go chase their trap?"

"Sure," he said, scuffing some of the salt under his boots. "Send me the location."

"Done. Listen, man, work on this new case, give it some time and you'll forget all about the last one. This could be it."

But as he hung up his phone, he saw a vision of a girl wearing a wide-brimmed hat. She was outlined in the distance, in the desert valley, under the rising sun. The borders of shimmering light illuminated Sherry's face, smiling sweetly. Sherry…younger? Or was it Amanda?

**8**

———

# THE PAVILION

WALKING WAS A REFRESHING CHANGE FOR AMANDA'S behind. As much as she loved driving the open road, she enjoyed this day of rest even more. Plus it was absolutely lovely outside. The blue sky was clear with just a few wisps of white, it was warm, and the air was still. She had even dressed in a summery outfit, with a wide-brimmed white hat, a white T-shirt, and leggings.

She had spent most of the early morning at the Denver zoo. Then she had headed to the botanical gardens. Now it was getting late and about time for her to head back to her hotel.

As she meandered along the grass, heading back to her car, she glanced with interest at a white-columned structure. The sun was dipping behind the horizon and it'd be dark soon. She'd have to return to her hotel, but the building was inviting. It was a Greek-columned structure. Amanda had always liked Greek architecture.

Inside a young couple was goofing off, pushing and pulling each other into their arms with their voices echoing. Otherwise it was vacant. They stopped their antics as soon as she walked up the steps. Then they ran off into the park.

She gazed back at the view of the grassy fields. Light over the horizon was turning a yellow hue. The view was perfect. She heaved a long sigh and took out her cell phone for a photo.

"The best view is in City Park."

Amanda gasped and whirled around. There was a man standing there wearing all black. He wore sunglasses and had a leather jacket draped over his shoulder. He was so still by one of the columns that she hadn't noticed him.

*Holy shit. It's my dark stranger!*

"I didn't mean to startle you."

"Are you following me?" She reached into her purse for her mace.

"The park's public. I come here for sunsets all the time. It's a pleasant view."

"Then why'd you say City Park is better?"

"It's an even better spot."

He came closer, but Amanda backed up. He seemed to take the cue and returned to his column. Then he nodded at the view. "I love this place." He dipped down his shades and glared at her. If it had been another man, she would have been frightened. Not him. Not with those angel eyes. "Wasn't it enough, Amanda, for you to nearly get into a car accident? Or have your window broken? Why didn't you go home like I warned?"

"How do you even know my name?"

"You told it to me."

"I never did. I'm sure I didn't."

She came closer. She didn't know why, but she did. Though he was intimidating, she felt safe with him.

"Do you live in Denver?" she asked.

"I live back where I saw you. But I travel a lot." Then he pointed at her. "You don't. You need to go home."

"Well, I shouldn't be talking to you then." She flashed a sly grin. "My mom told me to never talk to strangers."

"I'm hardly a stranger." Then he gestured to the park. "This park is haunted, you know. There's a thousand dead bodies under the ground. Sometimes when it rains, people claim to see skulls and bones. It used to be a cemetery. Did you know that?"

"You can be so creepy. Are you trying to scare me?" But she found herself closer to him. "I'm not afraid of you."

"Be afraid and go home, Amanda." He looked down at her, because she was right beside him and he was nearly a head taller. He looked at her through his shades, stern as hell. "Go home. Fly home."

"I won't," she said shaking her head, looking up. "Not until you tell me how you know my name."

"You said it to me when we first met."

"I didn't." She took her sunglasses off. She felt like taking her glasses off would get him to take off his so she could see those sea-blue gems. But he didn't. "I didn't. What's your name, anyway?"

"John."

Then, before she could say another word, he raised a finger. He touched his fingers, one at a time, as if counting. The light on the ceiling lit up. "I wish it didn't turn on so early."

"You're so weird, you know that?"

He nodded. "Yeah. Come on. Let's talk and walk—on the way back to your car."

"Why should I trust you?"

"Why are you alone in a city park? Did you know this place can be dangerous at night? I'd think you'd have learned about danger by now. Come." He pushed himself off the column. "Take a walk with me back to your car. If I were here to harm you, I could have done it last night."

"Gee, that makes me feel better."

"I'm not always good with words."

"Yeah, you don't seem to be the type that uses them."

He shrugged.

"I love words," Amanda said. "I'm a writer. I even have my own podcast. I want to be a journalist." She flashed a silly grin, then hated herself for it. It seemed so juvenile. He just nodded solemnly. Then he walked down the steps and turned. With his black leather jacket slung over one shoulder, he used his other hand to reach out for Amanda's. Amanda didn't take it. But she did walk down the steps with him.

"You said it was dangerous here at night," Amanda said.

"I told you you'd be safe with me."

"What about muggers?"

"Or ghosts? You'll be safe with me, Amanda. And after we talk, you can drive to the hotel, take a cab, and fly home."

But as they walked, the weirdest thing was he didn't say a word. With his shades and, at times, what appeared to be a scowl, he scanned the park. He had talked self-assuredly about them being safe, but he seemed to be looking everywhere for danger. He reminded her of a bodyguard or a secret agent or something. It was as if she were the president and he were a member of the secret service. He even gently put a hand on her back and guided her in the right direction on the walkway.

"Do you ever say anything, John?"

"No." But he added a hint of a smile. That made her laugh.

She actually didn't mind that she was walking with a quiet, handsome man. Not at all. Nor did she mind the direction the stranger was taking her. They were almost back to her car.

"Well, I kinda liked it when you talked in that Greek

building," she said. "I'd rather you talk. I like that. Can you say something to me?"

"That building is called The Pavilion."

"Yeah… Okay, that's something. How about I ask you something?"

"Go ahead."

She chuckled because he was so deadpan. Then he resumed scanning their surroundings.

"Why, or I should ask how, the hell did you fix my window?"

"Those assholes had no right to smash it. If they had touched you, I would have smashed them."

"Didn't you? Didn't you *smash them*?"

"I disabled their vehicle."

"That was nice, and thanks, but—" She turned and he was looking right at her. Even through the shades, it made her pause for a moment. "But…how did you get my window fixed so fast? And how did you get into my car in the first place?"

"I know people who can do it. I like cars. And it's not hard to get into yours, Amanda."

"Okay, see, that's creepy again."

"You should rightfully be afraid of me," he said with a nod. He put his thumbs in his pockets. "Most people are. But you're not, are you?"

"I don't like how quiet you are. But no, I feel safe around you."

"You're not safe."

She stopped walking and put her head down. For some reason, that really bothered her. She felt protected whenever she was with him, but there was something so off. Something really frightening.

"What's the matter?" he asked.

"Who are you?" she said, looking down and shaking her head. "Please. Tell me. Not the window." She clenched her fists. "Not Denver. Tell me about your car. Tell me why you're following me. It'll make me feel better."

"Now or in Arizona?"

"Whenever!" she snapped, looking up at his gaze. "And take those fucking glasses off for a second, won't you!"

He removed his shades. He had the loveliest eyes she had ever seen. They were glowing light blue. Gentle, which was juxtaposed to his appearance. Then she thought she understood why he wore them. His countenance seemed sad. And he had bags under his eyes, as if he never slept.

"In Arizona, a messenger came down to take your soul, Amanda. She is a lamia. *Lamia* is an ancient name for a monster that eats children. She's that kind of evil. She is called Lilith. But taking babies is a myth. Lilith takes souls. I chased her from you. But she managed to nearly collide with your car in the process, on a bike on the highway. Ever since then, ever since Arizona, you've been marked. You're at most risk on the road. The longer I can keep you away from the highway, the more likely they will stop bothering you. But they love battling on the open road. That's why I told you to go home by plane after I fixed your car. Here, in Denver, I'm protecting you. Though it's unlikely they'll hunt you in the middle of a city, they don't like cities, but they could approach you even here. Then they could follow you, like they did in Mesa Verde."

"Jesus, that's a mouthful," she said, wide-eyed. *Maybe it was better when he didn't say anything.* "Messengers? What does that mean?"

"Messengers. Watchers. We've also been called angels."

"Angels? Like heaven and God angels?"

"Angels," he said with a nod.

"And you're stalking me 'cause an angel is chasing me?"

He nodded.

"You're nuts, aren't you?" she asked with a nod, trying

to convince herself. Then she just resumed walking, though a little faster.

They were near the parking lot. When she made her way around a tree, she saw her car. But parked by her green VW was his super-expensive black sports car.

"How did you know my name, mister?" she asked, whirling around to face him again. "Hmm? And why are you following me?"

"Forget everything I said," he said in a too-measured voice. "You're right. I made all that shit up. I'm just some rich freak that's following you because I'm attracted to you. But I did scare off those guys near Grand Junction. Remember? I think that should allow me a little fun telling you my fantasy."

She squinted at him. Then she shook her head. No, he was quite serious about his "fantasy."

He put his shades back on. She didn't. The sun had fallen under the horizon.

"I have something to show you," he said. "I told you the view wasn't as great back there. I can show you better."

"What!" she snapped. She turned from him and looked down. Then she shook her head. "I'm sorry. I didn't mean to act angry with you."

"Why are you sorry?" he asked with a chuckle. He gently touched her chin. "Only you are kind enough to say sorry to a man causing you pain. Come on. I have something that will make seeing me again worth it. It's right near here. It'll be a better photo op. Believe me."

"Thought you said you were bringing that car to a client?" And she found herself smirking at him. Then he took his shades off again and she felt lost in those eyes.

"I lied."

He didn't explain any further. Instead he walked back to his luxury car. Amanda got in her VW Bug. That's when she noticed that his vehicle wasn't marked. There was no license plate.

Amanda shuffled in her pocket and brought out her recorder. She nearly dropped it.

"Guys, okay, I… I… I found that man I was talking about in Arizona again in Denver. I think he's following me. He's freaky, creepy, spooky—like, scary as hell, vampire-like shit or something. But he's hot. I mean, actually, he's really hot. And he's asking me to follow him… And he acts like he likes me. And I mean… so… should I? I mean, if he was following me, why would he ask me to follow *him*? Right?" Amanda watched him make his way slowly out of the parking lot. At the stop sign, he stopped his car. "Danger? Check. Well…if you don't hear from Caligirl gettingold24 again, it's been nice knowing all of you."

9
___________

# DENVER

They parked in an empty parking lot near a glass building not far from another city park. He reached out again for her hand. She still didn't take it. She walked close beside him though. This windowed building was the museum she had seen in the distance when she went to the zoo this morning.

The sound of two bicyclists made her jump as they rushed by. She was so on edge. Because he was so weird. She welcomed his presence, but there was this cringy unsettled feeling that brought back memories of the whole shattered-window-in-the-car thing.

In the distance was a gorgeous man-made lake with a waterfall. At this time, it was quiet and empty around the museum. She stopped to breathe it all in. And in the distance a lovely orange hue from the falling sun was beautifully shining over the water.

"Come on," John said, tugging her elbow. "It's better this way."

John took her to the front of the building, but he took a sharp left. He went around to the side. There he checked the handle to a glass door. It was unlocked. He opened it for her.

"Aren't we supposed to buy tickets or something?"

He shook his head. "EVS locks this door late every night. It'll be open for a couple hours."

"Aren't we gonna get arrested for trespassing?"

He shrugged.

*Oh, that's reassuring.*

"It'll be worth it. Trust me."

*Trust him. Hmm. Well, I suppose if I hadn't trusted him I would never have followed him. Why do you trust him, anyway, Amanda? Is it his chiseled chin? His wonderfully short dark hair? His bulging chest and arms under his T-shirt. His bright blue eyes. Why does he hide them? What a crime.*

Whoever or whatever this John was, he knew this Denver museum. He walked as if he were a tour guide, turning at just the right hallway and moseying his way down the dark corridors. He stopped at an elevator. It looked very plain, like a service elevator. They exited at the top floor. Then another walk through a hallway beside glass windows, and outside onto an outdoor patio. And then—

*Holy shit!*

Amanda ran to the ledge of a wide balcony. She felt giddy. The sun was down, but the rays shone behind the mountains, casting a gold hue over the buildings of downtown.

"What did I tell you?"

She looked at him and nodded. Then she fumbled in her jeans pocket for her old mini-recorder. She turned back to the view, leaned on the rail, and clicked the record button.

"Umm...so here I am before this view of downtown Denver, Colorado. There's birds chirping, it's quiet, nobody's out because it's late. But that stranger I told you guys about is with me now. Say hi, stranger." And she pointed the recorder at John. John furrowed his brow, gazing at Amanda, looking as if she was crazy. "Hmm?" Amanda said, pointing the recorder at his face again. "Go ahead. Don't be shy. Say hi."

"Hi," he said into the device.

"He says his name is John," she said into the recorder with a chuckle. "He's mysterious as hell. Nice though." She gazed at him from head to toe with a smile. He continued to look at her like she was nuts. That made her laugh again. "We're at the top of, like, this modern glass building in City Park, and I can see the buildings of the city. They've got all their lights shining. And it's so pretty. How can I describe it? The sun's gone, but rays are shining behind the mountains, casting a gorgeous gold hue over the high rises. Even the green grass below the park surrounding the lake is pretty, with an orange glow over the water beside a forest green. It's…breathtaking. I couldn't be at a better place anywhere. Or with—" Her gaze turned from the vista to John. He didn't smile. "It's…" Then she couldn't find the words. God, had she become tongue-tied? She'd never had that happen before. "It's…this is what my trip is all about, folks. And my new friend, John, showed it to me. But now I have to go, take a few pics of Denver, and thank him. I tell you, this is what cross-country trips are all about. This is what it's… Shit, I already said all that, didn't I?" She laughed. She took a deep breath and sighed. "Damn." Then she clicked off her recorder.

She leaned on the rail and took another deep breath.

"That's for my fans," she said, cocking her head back at him. She didn't look at him, but she chuckled remembering his deadpan expressions. "I run a podcast. That's why I went on this cross-country disaster. You know, log all the stuff for my listeners. I want to be a journalist. So I figured the best way to land a great job was to get out there and show people what I've got. Go on vacation and log all my unknowns to people. I mean, that's what news is. It's about telling people cool stuff in a cool way. Right? This whole cross-country thing is unknown to me. Obviously, not to you. So I thought, why not add something to my podcast? And you never know, I could make money off my little traveling show. I already spoke about amazing tortillas and enchiladas in Tucson, the cliffs at Mesa Verde, and the fricking Denver zoo. It's amazing, you know? Do you understand?"

He shrugged.

"Now I'm on to talking about you to my fans, the weirdest guy of all."

He didn't say a word. And she laughed at that. She turned back to the beautiful vista. "Why'd you take me here? Huh?"

"You liked the view at the Pavilion."

"Yeah." She nodded with a sigh. "But you're right. This is better."

"I come here a lot."

"That doesn't surprise me. You're a drifter. Like a yuppie drifter. Right? That's what you said. A rich guy with a pretty car that drives for the hell of it. Right?" She chuckled at his expressionless nod. Then she reached in her pocket for her cell phone. First she used it for her reflection to shake her long blond hair out and fix it for the shot. Then she turned the phone with an extended arm to get a good selfie.

"You want me to take a picture of you?" he asked.

"Oh, could you?"

He grabbed her cell phone and she posed by the rail.

"Hey, why don't we get one together?" she asked.

For some really weird reason, he hesitated. But then he nodded and stood beside her. He put an arm around her, and his fingers left tingles along her back.

*Calm down, Amanda. You're acting like a man's never touched you.*

She had him in the picture on her phone. But then she jerked away.

"Take your sunglasses off, weirdo!"

He obliged, but he didn't seem like he wanted to. Then he posed with her again. After a couple snaps, and a glance at their pictures on the phone, she turned back to him. "It's not…" she stammered, looking deep into his eyes. There was a hint of a smile on his face. "Why…why do you cover that?"

"Cover what?"

"Your eyes?" she asked, exploring them. "They're so nice. Why do you cover them?"

He didn't answer. Instead he did something far better. He leaned down and gently touched his lips to hers. Then he stroked her cheek with a single finger.

"Thank you," she breathed.

He chuckled. That made her laugh too.

"Got you to laugh. I knew I could!" She turned back to the view. "Oh, it's just so pretty here. Thank you, John. I love views. That's why I love driving so much. I'm from LA, you know, and my favorite thing is to drive where you can't see the end of the horizon. LA always has some hill or building in your way. I saw my first great view in the desert when I first met you. Then when I entered Colorado, it was flats till the mountains. But the Rockies here are pretty too. I love traveling and experiencing places I've never been. Even the smells—aside from your cologne—which I don't mind. I mean, it's nice. There's even a park smell here. You know, mainly the grass, I suppose. And there's a lovely gentle breeze. Do you feel it? It's nice. It's a lovely night."

"Yes, it is," he said, leaning on the rail. Then he put his sunglasses back on.

She furrowed her brow.

"So…you're in town," she said. "Have you eaten? I'm sure if you can show me this, you can point me somewhere good to eat for dinner? We could eat?"

He nodded. But he weirdly didn't answer her.

"You sure knew this place," she said. "Can I ask how many times you've been up here?"

"You don't want to know."

"Okay, that sounds weird."

"I know."

"'Cause you're some kind of protector of souls, protecting them from angels?" She looked back at the view but cocked her head back at him.

He nodded solemnly.

"I know you're not just a rich yuppie in a sports car. I get it. You just don't want to tell me what you're really doing. It just made me feel better when I said that."

He just nodded again.

Before she could inquire further, his phone rang. He gestured with a raised finger and crossed the walkway alone. She gazed back at the view but watched him from the corner of her eye. From his expression, she couldn't tell if he was ordering a pizza or talking about a friend dying in the hospital. Then he put the phone back in his jeans pocket.

"I have to go, Amanda," he said. She pouted and there was a hint of amusement on his lips. "I need you to do me a favor while I'm away."

"Anything, handsome."

"Go home." He walked right up to her. He removed his shades, looking grave. "Go. Please, by plane from Denver. Don't drive. Go now. That's why I came to see you again. You have to go home."

But she came right up to his face, stood on her tippytoes, and planted her lips on the stubble of his cheek. Her lips glided down with more kisses until landing on his lips again. His arm curled around her back as she swooned.

"When will you be back?" she breathed.

"I can't," he said quietly. "I can't. Go. Please."

But then he leaned down and kissed her lips again.

"No," she said, shaking her head. "I don't want to leave."

She wouldn't let go of him. She kissed him again. She felt his tongue enter her mouth and run along hers. And for the longest time, they just kissed. His arms held her tighter. And she was lost. And she wanted to be lost in his embrace like this for good.

"Oh, John."

"Go home, please," he pleaded. He gently pushed away from her.

"Sorry, can't do that to my fans," she said with a giggle.

"It's not funny," he said, looking angry for the first time. "I'll take you back to your car and watch you get back to your hotel safely. Then I want you to fly home."

She looked down at his hand hesitantly. She slowly shook her head. Then she snatched his hand and came really close to him again and kissed him. She pressed herself into his arms.

"*Go!*" he shouted, pushing her angrily from him. "Go home!"

She jumped in reaction to his rage.

"Look, you seem like a cool guy, okay," Amanda snapped back, "but I'm not going to go buy a ticket and jump on a plane just because you say it's not safe to drive!"

"If you don't believe what I've told you, tell me why you've been in so much danger?"

"I've been told it can be dangerous to travel alone."

She smiled and then, as he remained stern, she laughed.

"Come on, John, a near accident and a couple drunk

vandals?" She put her hand on her hips and shrugged. "No. Honestly, the only thing weirding me out on my trip is you."

She waited for a reply. Anything. After nothing but silence, she headed back to the elevator, with or without him.

She didn't want to. She wanted to jump in his arms before the view of downtown Denver again. Kissing him. She could have done that for another hour. But that moment seemed ruined.

He followed her inside the elevator without another word. Yet, as angry as he seemed, he stood close beside her. And she felt his hand brush against hers. And it was, again, weird. It was as if the closer she came to him, the more he was repelled. It was as if she were poison. But it seemed he wanted the poison as much as she did.

"Thanks for showing me the view."

## 10

## THE MESSAGE

THE FIRST THING THAT JOHN NOTICED AS HE ENTERED THE
motel room was the rusty stench of iron mixed with excre-
ment. Then he saw red. The beige motel carpet was
riddled with crimson blotches that trailed all the way from
the door to the bed. John's pale-skinned boss, Raphael,
known simply as Rick, stood over the white sheets wearing
shades just like John's. And he wore identical black clothes.
The sheets were drenched in red. And in the middle of a
bloody puddle a naked dark-skinned woman lay on her
side. The head was mercifully turned away from the door.
As John approached, he noticed her abdomen was split
open, body curling around coils that looked like snakes. He
recognized the crimson snakes as her intestines. The
stomach had been splayed open. And her legs were severed
at her thighs.

John made his way to the other side of the bed and saw
blood still dripping from the woman's fingertips. Then he
saw that her face, her profile, was no longer identifiable.

"Angel's down," Rick said bitterly. "Tori. She was nineteen, Black, with long black hair. She went to Boise Univer-

sity." Rick held her limp wrist. "She was studying sociology. Born a Leo. They opened her up. Filleted her."

"How long till the police come?"

"An hour or so. No one knows much about this except us. She doesn't have family or many friends. She was ambushed on her way to her date on Interstate Eighty-Four." Rick touched her hand. Then he touched the dripping, bloody finger. "It was very recent." Rick ran his finger along one of the only white sections of the sheet to wipe off the blood. Then he looked up at John. "I had a case in Belize with Samael. I couldn't get here in time to save this angel. But you could have. You were close. After the initial call, I called you again. You ignored my messages. You didn't take my call until it was too late."

"I was detained."

"Bullshit." Rick finally faced John, shaking his head and looking pissed.

"I've answered every job for years."

"Well, you can fucking live with this one." Rick dug his finger into his chest. "Her death is on you."

Rick brooded for a moment. Then he walked back to the face and turned the head toward him—her eyes being the only thing recognizable on her face. All other features were too bloodied. Knife wounds running down from both cheeks splayed the opening of her mouth unnaturally wide. Even her nose was severed. "Look at her. Look at this face. She's dead because of you."

"Oh, fuck off, Raphael. If they die, perhaps they're in a better place than we are."

"You were so close, man!" Then he looked for more "clean" sheets to wipe his hand again. "So close. What the hell are you doing? Falling into their trap? This final test is your fault. You looked too deep into your past. End your interest in the girl. You're the best operative I've ever had. You want to fuck up when you're so damn close to being done? You think Michael's gonna let you ascend now? Don't you get it? That's precisely why this Amanda bitch was put on your path. You know she's a trap. Don't you care? If not for your soul, how about Amanda's? And these other ones you're ignoring? You don't get it. You don't do my job, you'll be doing theirs. There is no both ways. It's either me or them. Lilith knows she can use Amanda to draw you away from me."

"Lilith told me Amanda would be chased again in Colorado."

"So what? You think you're in love? Is that it, John? She's not Sherry. Fuck, she's not her. She's Amanda. Amanda's gonna be just like this body within a year whether you fucking help her or not. If they don't get her now, Lilith or Samael will get her later. Meanwhile as you're screwing around, more of these bodies are going to pile up in every seedy motel across the country." He used his pale hand to pick up her head again. "This girl. Look at her. Tori was her name. Damn it, look at her!"

John turned away.

"*Fucking look at her!* This girl, Tori was her name, could have lived, like your girlfriend, for another year or two. But you traded her life for a goddamn date!"

"I don't need this shit right now." John walked to the door. Rick touched his shoulder, and John raised his fist to him.

"John," Rick said, quickly raising a hand, "her body was filleted. Legs were severed. They didn't just kill her. This was a message. Usually it's a noose or throat cut. If you get personal, they'll use it to damn you. They're fucking with your head."

"How is this a message?"

"The mutilation damages her chance of a proper burial," he replied with a shrug.

"Oh come on."

"You can't bury a body in pieces properly, John."

"Ashes to ashes, dust to dust," John said, shaking his head. "This angel's soul will ascend."

"Well, you won't. The mutilation is a personal message for you." He came up to his face and pointed a finger at him. "Is Amanda really worth losing your soul? You're being judged. This is the toughest, but speaking as your chief and friend, you've gotta come around on this."

John turned. Rick touched his arm, and John yanked it off.

"John, the next one's name is Carly. She's forty-two with short black hair. She's driving to Miami tomorrow. She's a Virgo."

"Are you serious?" he asked, removing his shades and staring at him.

"Move on," Rick said with a stern nod. "Let Amanda go."

John grabbed the doorknob. "Fuck you."

"Fuck!" Rick cried, "I'm not even sure this has anything to do with Amanda! I think you're washed up, man. Lilith already got to your head in Vegas, didn't she? Both heads."

"Fine, consider me washed up."

"They're going to extend your time. No proper burial for her, no proper burial for you. No ascension. Your soul will be damned if you keep letting people die. Your soul will be forfeit. That's the message. Stop thinking of yourself and think of these victims."

"I got the message."

He headed for his car in the parking lot.

"If you don't answer your call, I'll be needing your keys," Rick cried out. "I warn you, if you're grounded, we're done. It isn't my decision. One more death like this, and you'll get even more time here on Earth. You'll be removed. I remember how you talked about Amanda.

You're smitten with the girl version of your former lover. Lilith is mixing up your mind. I tell you, the broad's not Sherry. Leave Amanda. Leave her."

John opened the door to his car.

"The new angel down is Carly, John. She's forty-two with—"

John showed him his middle finger.

"Angel down, John!" Raphael yelled. "Miami. *Not fucking Kansas!*"

**11**

———

# KANSAS

AMANDA GAZED THROUGH HER WINDSHIELD AT THE RISING sun, the surrounding clouds splashing yellowish orange, as light rose over a short plateau off the horizon. The infinite vista was like water off the shore back home, only this wasn't the ocean. It was miles upon miles of farmland. Her land. She felt like a pioneer. She was the driver, and behind the wheel, the whole world was hers. She sipped her nitro brew reflecting on that. Then she put her clear plastic cup, filled with the wonderful elixir, back in her cup holder. But…she didn't like that. Before her window was broken, her cup holder had been full of gum wrappers and trash. The lack of clutter reminded her of her nightmare.

She had a flashback of glass shattering in the side window.

*Turn on music. Get your mind off of it, Mandi.*

So she did. She put on Journey. As she tapped on her steering wheel, Steve Perry's voice, and the now-bright sun over the lovely vista, made her feel better. Then her eyes fell on the passenger seat—her replacement cactus, her only companion. It was vibrating as she drove down the empty highway.

By the time she was on her third Journey album, it became overcast. That reminded her of all those documentaries she used to watch about tornadoes. She loved tornado hunter shows. But not now. She wouldn't mind seeing one far off in the distance though—in the very far distance, not beside her car.

She exited onto an off-ramp at a gas station. It was lunchtime. She pumped gas and then walked over to a small diner beside the gas station.

"What'll it be?" asked an overweight guy in suspenders by her table. He pointed to the small menu on the table and winked.

"Do you still serve breakfast? I'd love a bacon and cheese omelet."

"Sure." He nodded. "Where're you from?"

"Los Angeles."

"Los Angeles? I've got a sister in Malibu. You live out on the beach?"

"Santa Monica," she said, shaking her head. She chuckled. "I mean, it's close to the beach, I suppose."

"On vacation?"

She nodded.

"You'd like anything to drink with your eggs?"

"A cup of coffee would be nice."

"Cup of Joe. You betcha. I'll be back soon."

*Cup of Joe. Cute.*

He winked and headed for the kitchen. Most of the café booths were empty. So she pulled out her small recorder.

"Guys," she said quietly, "I'm at a diner in Kansas. Can you fucking believe that? The waiter is sooo nice. I'm gonna eat an omelet at one p.m. cause…why the hell not? I've got a view of wheat and grass fields. That's all there is. It's like a sea of green. And I'm already liking it. I mean, I had Steve Perry with me in the car."

She clicked the recorder off.

She looked over at the people pumping gas. That's when she noticed a very distinctive woman by one of the gas tanks wearing all black, too black, pumping gas with a black-gloved hand into a pitch-black motorcycle. She kept her helmet and opaque visor on, but she wore a white scarf around her neck that matched the long white hair trailing down her back—very white hair. As she waited to fill her tank, she stood folding her arms. Then she scared Amanda by gazing right in her direction.

The waiter brought over her cup of coffee. Amanda gladly looked away.

"You get tornadoes here?" she asked.

"Hope not," he said with a smirk. "I haven't seen a twister in these parts in a long while. Plenty of wind though. Watch what you wish for, miss."

"I figured it'd be like seeing surfers on the beach in California," she said with a chuckle.

"Only in the movies."

The biker was still staring at the diner. That was so weird. Especially because she must have been done pumping gas.

*Is this the danger John was talking about?*

But then she remembered the glass windows of the diner were tinted. The woman could just be staring at the restaurant, not at her. She did her best to ignore her.

After Amanda's omelet lunch and a second cup of coffee, the biker outside had, thankfully, disappeared. Amanda checked her phone. It was one-thirty. Her plan was to get to Kansas City, or at least Topeka, by nightfall.

Back behind the wheel, she enjoyed the open road again. It was pretty empty—except for the motorcycle. That black leather–clad biker had reappeared and was following her.

Two semis slowed down traffic, blocking both lanes.

Amanda breathed a big sigh of relief when the biker quickly zoomed around her and between the two trucks. She zoomed off into the distance.

After another five miles in the clear, she leaned back in her seat and pulled out her tape recorder from her pocket, turned down the radio, took a deep breath, and—

"Guys, I'm loving this view. It's awesome. Or, resplendent. I'm a Caligirl, so when I'm driving off in the desert or plains looking at sunsets or zooming past hilltops with an endless horizon, my mouth is, like, totally dropping. The beach is great but the desert horizon is to-die-for. And as I'm getting into Kansas, I've got grasslands forever, which is just as good. It's like totally Dorothy. Honestly, I'm still glad I took this trip—even after that death-defying danger I told you about."

Amanda drove past another slow semi. She spotted the weird motorcyclist, in the distance, thankfully—a mile or so ahead now. It was hard to judge distance with the flat horizons. She clicked the recorder back on.

"Let's check off what I've seen so far, shall we—oh, and each comes with a photo on my website, of course:

Saguaros, check.

Speeding over a hundred miles an hour (maybe, but that'd be illegal (wink). You can just guess).

Sampling Starbucks in every state, check, check (lattes taste the same everywhere!)

Sunrises over the Great Basin, check.

Pueblo village in caves, check.

Dark handsome man with shades. Check.

Dark handsome man showing me a view of Denver at sunset. Check.

Dark handsome man kissing me over the view of Denver. Check. Check.

Dark handsome man holding me in his arms… Okay, you get the picture.

Danger?… Yep, a bit too much. Love? Check. Check. Check."

She pressed stop.

Amanda jumped when her music changed to a ringing phone. She touched the phone button on her console.

"Hey, Mands. Just checking in. I gave you a day off. How's your trip?"

"Fuck, you scared me, Lu."

"Sorry. How's the trip?"

"Great, Lu."

"Did you make a decision about next month?"

"What decision?"

"Come on! Cut it out. I have to know."

Amanda froze. As she had passed a bridge overpass, two more black bikes with black-leather riders had appeared behind her. Then the black bike ahead in the other lane had slowed, letting her pass. Now three bikes were trailing behind her.

"Well?" asked Luane. "Can we or not? Ben's ready to break up with me for waiting so long. Really babe, I have to know. He has to know so he can decide on renting the place or not."

"I don't know, Lu," Amanda muttered, staring at the bikes in her rearview mirror. "What if you break up with Benji and we're left out in the cold."

"That won't happen."

"You just said you were fighting." Amanda kept talking to stall. Because she didn't want to scare her again.

"The mountains aren't cold in the summer," Luane said. "You said that yourself. And we can buy a tent if the place doesn't work out. We won't get stranded."

"Okay, Luane. Fine."

"Okay? Really! Okay? Love you, babes! Hey…how many more days do you got driving around the world? When will you be back?"

"Just a few more. It's so pretty in Kansas. But the clouds are graying."

"As long as you don't drive through a tornado."

"This guy in a diner told me they don't have that many tornadoes here."

"There's like a hundred a year in Kansas, Mands. Oh, before I forget, I got more good news for you."

"What?"

The bikers were swaying back and forth, swerving pompously from lane to lane, in a pack behind her. Their bikes were so black that they stuck out on the two-lane highway. They reflected the sun like black jade. They were alone on the highway now. But that wasn't comforting. It reminded her of Colorado. What did they want? If they wanted to break her window, they would have done it already.

"Are you mad?" asked Luane.

"What? Mad about what?"

"Aren't you even listening to me, Mandi? I said, I opened your mail. I couldn't resist. You got an interview, babe."

"No way! Where?"

"Phoenix. They want you in Phoenix next week. Guess you'll be off driving again."

"No way!" Amanda said again. She stared at the console as if Luane were in the car. "Hey, wait a minute! What the hell were you doing opening my mail?"

"See. That's why I asked if you were mad."

"Oh, I thought you meant crazy, as in I'm insane."

"No, I already know you're crazy. I meant angry. But I saw the formal letter and I thought it was one of *my* applications."

"Phoenix. That'd be so awesome."

"I know, right? You won't be some spinster waiting on some hot guy to pay your rent."

"That's one of my top jobs, Lu."

"Mine too."

"Nothing for you, yet?"

"Nope."

One of the bikes approached Amanda's driver's side window. A man seemed to be studying her and her car through his tinted visor. He signaled something to the woman rider behind. Then he fell back with the other two bikers. Then the three bikes trailed close, too close, tailgating her car.

"You know…" Luane was still jibber-jabbering. "If I get a job there, we can room together again. I've got a lot of hopes in Phoenix. But even if I get something back here, we won't be that far apart. I say do your best. Take the job, whatever it takes, Mands. We'll see."

Amanda glanced at her rearview mirror. She couldn't believe her eyes. On the far horizon behind her, a black streak was approaching at an incredible speed. A car? John? Her heart sped in excitement; all morning she had been filled with dread over losing him. But somehow she'd known she'd see him again. Now she felt a queer mix of relief and fear. For it meant…

*Shit. I'm in trouble again.*

"I think I have to go, Lu."

"Oh. Okay. Thought you were bored in Kansas."

*No. Not exactly bored.*

It was her dark stranger for sure. His car had become definable about two miles back. And in another second, he was right behind the three bikes.

The female biker with white hair and a white scarf was in the center. She gave some hand signal to the other bikers. Two of the bikes split off and ended up beside Amanda's car. One was in the fast lane; the other was driving on the right shoulder. Then the ringleader-lady rode in front of Amanda's car and slammed on her brakes.

*"Shit!"*

Amanda pressed hard on her brakes, and her car swayed left to right, losing control for a moment. She came an inch away from hitting the biker in front of her. Then a bike on Amanda's left came dangerously close, forcing her to veer toward the shoulder. She thought she was going to hit the bike on her right, but that motorcycle had already fallen back again. Then John crashed his car into the white-haired woman biker. The biker lost balance for a moment, shaking like crazy, but then somehow, impossibly, recovered on the highway. Then all three bikes were back to riding behind her, swerving left to right, as if nothing had happened, seemingly taunting both her and John.

John crashed into the biker again. The impact was hard enough to throw the motorcycle in front of Amanda's car, and she had to swerve to avoid hitting it. But somehow the biker recovered, pulled back, and came right next to Amanda's passenger window. She pounded on the glass with a gloved fist and shouted something. Amanda couldn't understand the words because before the biker could hit her glass again, John hit her once more.

But then another biker came dangerously close to Amanda's driver's side. This one didn't bother with her window; he just rammed his bike into her car.

Amanda found herself pushed toward the shoulder. In front of her, John slammed on his brakes, and the motorcycle ramming Amanda was hurled back. Then her VW was hit by a third bike. She didn't see the collision coming. She felt it.

She lost control and her car spun off the highway, running right into the green wheat fields. She tried the brakes, but her car launched over a ditch and a dirt road. Then she came to a stop in the middle of the wheat field. One of the bikers was waiting. He leaped off his bike, still wearing his helmet, and ran toward her. Behind him, on the far-off horizon behind the freeway, John's black car was still battling the two motorcycles. As the biker moved closer to her hood, Amanda hit the gas, plowing into him. Then she pushed her car through the wheat, pressing her foot hard on the accelerator.

She merged onto a dirt road adjacent to the freeway. She looked back and her assailant was still lying on the ground near his bike in the wheat field. She might have run over him.

She speeded back onto the freeway. Then, like she had done in the middle of the night in Colorado, she drove at the fastest speed she could manage. And, luckily, her car wasn't damaged enough to stop her.

She rapidly passed a large truck. The trucker was wide-eyed with horror. But he wasn't paying any attention to her. He was watching the bedlam between John and the other two bikers ahead. They kept ramming each other.

She nearly caught up to John and the two bikes. That was because more cars were appearing up ahead, forcing them to slow down. She looked in her rearview mirror for the third biker. Thankfully, he was gone.

Then, perhaps the weirdest, most normal thing happened. A police car pulled up behind her. She saw red and blue lights flashing and then heard sirens. She would gladly pull over. The officer said something through a megaphone, but he only said a couple words. The remaining male biker rode full force into the police car, causing it to launch off the freeway like she had. But the impact made the biker ricochet into the central concrete barricade.

The motorcyclist started his bike again behind her.

*How!*

Then he came right behind Amanda again, doing that infernal leaning back and forth behind her. But the police officer was gone.

Traffic thickened. John and the demon lady had slowed down to a nearly normal freeway speed up ahead. They were heading into construction, and traffic in all the lanes were merging into a line of cars.

About a half mile ahead, the lady's bike squeezed beside John's car and rode on a thin shoulder. They approached a bridge. On the bridge, he squeezed his car on the thin shoulder behind her and slammed the girl biker hard. The crash was enough to send the biker over the concrete wall and into the river below.

Amanda's car was hit. The last biker had hit the back of her car.

She sped up but then had to slam on the brakes by the bridge. John turned his car around up ahead and drove backward along the right shoulder to catch up to her and the bike. He zoomed right past her passenger side.

When her car came to a stop by traffic on the bridge, the sole biker behind her got out of his bike. He brandished a gun and approached her passenger window. Then he pointed it at her. She screamed and covered her head.

*Bang.*

It was loud, but it wasn't a gunshot. A black blur on the shoulder rushed by the window. John must have collided full speed into her assailant's body.

After that, John pulled his car over where the construction ended. To wait for her?

The biker gang was gone. Her dark stranger had saved her again.

Amanda looked at her console. She gasped, remembering her friend.

*Lu! God, are you still on the phone?*

No, either she had hung up or Amanda, in the throes of chaos, had hung up on her.

Amanda waited for the traffic to open into two lanes. John's window was open. He gestured to talk to her. She didn't roll down hers. Instead, she weirdly drove with other cars at the speed limit—a "normal" speed again. John pulled up behind her VW and followed her.

There was a rest stop two miles ahead. John drove up to her side and pointed to it, but even as traffic cleared and the off-ramp was ahead, Amanda was too afraid to stop.

She drove for another half hour with John trailing her.

Soon they approached a small town. Amanda drove off one of the off-ramps by a gas station. John followed.

She pulled into the station, parked her car. Then she put her head in her hands. She was surprised that her eyes were wet. She had been crying. She didn't even know when the tears had fallen.

John pulled his black car into a space next to her. His door opened. She watched the dark man, his black pants and T-shirt and shades.

"Are they gone?" she asked. She realized she hadn't opened her car door or rolled down her window. He nodded, seeming to understand her.

"God, John, what's happening?" she asked, rolling down the window. "What's happening?"

"You're in shock," he said with a nod. "Come with me."

"I think I'd rather stay in my car."

He nodded.

Then he just put his fingers in his pants pockets and stared out onto the infinite horizon through his shades. He waited and she thought if she stayed in the car forever, he'd still be there waiting for her.

Slowly, she opened her door. When she stood up, she reached for him. He embraced her.

"It's over."

**12**

___

# A FAMILIAR TRAIL

THEY WALKED. SHE HAD NO IDEA WHERE BUT, SOMEHOW, her dark stranger seemed to know the way. Just like at the museum, he seemed to know every direction, even down this trail in the middle of nowhere. She let him hold her hand this time and lead her through bushes and then down a small slope onto a dirt road. The dirt path was beside rows of wheat. Like the highway, this road went on for miles in both directions. It seemed to go on forever—which she loved. But clouds were out, so it was gloomy.

"Are you feeling better?"

"No." She turned to him and flashed a grin. "I'm terrified. But at least you're with me."

"You're marked," he said with a nod. He looked down at her shoes and she followed his eyes to her sandals.

"I didn't expect to go walking," she said with a shrug.

"I don't think you expected a lot of things. We don't have to walk far. Walking helps get my mind off things. I do it a lot. I thought it'd help you."

"I don't mind. Why won't they leave me alone?"

"I told you, you're marked. If Lilith or her messengers find you, they'll terminate you. They will do this until you return home. Big cities, like Los Angeles, are safe. Denver's safe too, the highways between aren't. Your home is your best hideout. They'd rather do their jobs outside your home, away from the city. When you're alone. That's why I told you to fly home."

"It's too unbelievable to believe."

He nodded.

"Why me?"

"You're pure. Pure souls are deemed worthy of an early release to heaven."

"Pure?" She laughed. Then she shook her head. "That's funny. I'm not pure, John. Sorry, but boy, you've got the wrong girl on that one."

He shook his head.

"So what do *you* have to do with all this?" She was examining his face. "Hmm?" But he was wearing his infernal sunglasses. She couldn't read him.

"I'm protecting you." He resumed walking beside her. "Usually after the first fight, they leave targets alone. Lilith wants to torment you."

"Why am I the lucky girl?"

"Because I've been doing this job for too long." He heaved a long sigh and turned from her, looking at the infinite fields of wheat. Nothing he said really made much sense. He was the most closed-book guy she had ever met. "It's difficult to explain," he said, still staring at the horizon. "I only needed to save a few more souls to ascend. But Lilith met me in Vegas and warned me that she'd be after you. While I protect you, others die. And the punishment is far greater than the rewards I've accrued. Every soul that dies is worth many times more than the souls I've saved. So every couple days means months and months more time here as I watch over you."

"Then watch over the others, John," she said, shaking

her head and brushing her hand along his arm. He stared at her hand.

"The touch of an angel," he said quietly.

"I'm not, I tell you."

And she squeezed his hand. She felt him play with her fingers.

"We call the victims angels because of their purity," John said, gazing into her eyes through his shades. "Now that you're marked, you're an angel ready to ascend to heaven, like me, only sooner."

"Well, that really doesn't sound so bad."

"I realize it all sounds nuts. But certainly you believe me after everything that's happened to you?"

"Uh, yeah. I believe you."

"What else do you want to know? You deserve answers now."

"How old are you?"

He grew a smile. Finally. She loved that she could make him smile.

"I'd be twenty-eight."

"So you're alive?"

"Ah," he said, lifting an eyebrow. "I understand." But, of course, he didn't answer, and that was worse.

"Do you have a girlfriend?"

"No." And she was rewarded with a smile again.

"John, every question you answer leads to another. I don't get you. What's worse is you really don't say anything even when you talk. You just nod."

And he infernally nodded. Then he looked up at the sun behind a cloud. "It will be dark soon. Ask me anything you want. Then I can escort you to the next city and you can fly home and leave for good."

But she didn't want to say a thing after he said something dreadful like that.

They came upon water. It was probably a run-off for

the crops, but it was about ten feet across. John let go of her hand and stepped onto a pipe crossing the water. Then, while balancing his body with outstretched arms, he walked midway across. He reached for her.

"Are you crazy! Oh, no. Do you have any idea how clumsy I am?"

"I'll catch you."

"Nuh-uh. I'm wearing flip-flops. And if I fall, I'm gonna have all this dirt on my white shorts."

But he didn't take no for an answer. He reached out for her. She grabbed his hand. Then she closed her eyes and screamed as she stepped on the pipe. He guided her, but as she adjusted her balance, it nearly threw him over. She somehow made it across and landed in his arms. He laughed. She looked up into his face. *OMG.* He was so close.

"Why… I have another question… Why do you wear those sunglasses?"

He took them off. That was far worse. She got lost in his eyes. He leaned down and kissed her again and held her in his arms. He smelled good. Like vanilla. She liked his cologne. She brushed her hand along the stubble on his cheek.

"You have lovely eyes," she said between touching his lips. "Why do you cover them?" She realized she had stupidly closed hers.

"The light can be blinding."

She let that go. Because it sounded like another riddle. She looked away, toward the fields. It was getting more dark and stormy. Then she shook her head and headed down the walkway again.

"I'm special?" she asked. "I'm pure and innocent?"

He nodded.

"That's really fucking dumb. And, by the way, I emphasize the word *fucking*. There. I cussed. Fuck, fuck, fuck. I tell you, you've got the wrong fucking girl. I'm not innocent. And I'm hardly an angel."

"Michael doesn't make mistakes."

"Who the fuck is Michael?"

He brushed his hand over the tips of some wheat. Then he put his thumbs in his pockets. "I don't know exactly. He's an overseer. He's not really a person. He determines who is damned and who ascends. This world is an in-between world. Michael watches over all of us. And the messengers decide who ascends and who falls."

"I think you mean God."

"No. I don't believe in God."

"You're an angel, but you don't believe in God?" Her eyes widened. She laughed heartily. "Are you kidding? That is the most ridiculous thing I've ever heard. I tell you, John, it's almost as ridiculous as you calling me innocent."

"Michael is not an all-powerful being like God. If he were, I don't think there would be so much suffering in this world. He's a judge. And he determined that you must already ascend as a good angel and be sent to the next realm. He wants you to ascend so you can go to heaven."

"You said I was an 'angel down.'"

"Yes. An angel on this Earth in trouble. Every being on this planet is born angelic. When close to death, we call them fallen. "Angel down" is a code that means there is an angel that needs help. So far, Lilith has hunted you near the border. Then when I saved you, two angels near Grand Junction attacked you. Now in Kansas, angels, with Lilith in the lead, tried to kill you again. They hunt to kill you because you're marked to go to heaven early."

"What can I do to get unmarked?"

"You can't. Some live for a few more years. I need you to fly back before you ascend early." He turned from her and looked at the clouds. Then he stopped talking, which bothered her more. After a long silence, she said, "ascend?"

Then she gesticulated with her hand for him to explain, but he didn't say anything. He looked away. "As in, *die*. Why? Why would I *ascend* early."

"Those souls," he explained, "that are too pure no longer need to be tested. The world we live in is a test. We are between the states of heaven and hell. In ancient times, it was called purgatory. It's up to you, in your lifetime, to either ascend to heaven or be brought down to hell. Those that are too pure are deemed ready to be taken immediately. Those souls, like you, are rare. But there's no more need to test them. Have you ever wondered why the most angelic people die so early? They are taken and killed by angels."

"So you're protecting me from angels trying to kill me? If they take me, I die and go to heaven?"

"So they say."

"What in the hell is wrong with that?" She looked at him. Really examined him. "And if they're angels, what does that make you?"

He didn't answer. He looked more serious than ever.

She stopped and gazed at his black T-shirt and pants. His boots. His dark shades. Emotionless. He had a presence about him. A power. But he also reminded her of shadows. A vampire. Or darkness… Death. Death… Yes, he was like death. It reminded her of that creepiness she felt when they met in Colorado. Like that first meeting, when she thought she had gotten into a car crash and was going to…die. No, worse, he was death itself. And that's what he said she was destined for. Angels were trying to kill her. And every time her life was threatened, her dark stranger, her so-called guardian angel, appeared… Every time she was near death. Like a grim reaper or something.

She felt a lump in her throat. For the first time since she met him, she shook before him. She felt like she was in the presence of a devil—an entity that could harm her. Her eyes grew wide. She became afraid, just like in the car chase.

He put his hand up and shook his head.

"You're *dark*…you're *evil*, John. If you're fighting angels, you're a bad one."

He nodded. He actually nodded.

*What! What the hell?*

"You're evil," she repeated, as if trying to explain it to herself. "You're evil, John."

"Wait—"

She turned from him.

"Let me explain."

She would run back to the car. Crossing the pipe, she slipped and her leg fell knee deep into the water, of course. She cursed and blamed him for her soaking muddy feet. But she didn't stop running. She continued down their trail back to the gas station.

"Amanda!"

Her bare legs now drenched in mud and water, her sandals caked in mud, she picked up her pace, tripped on the dusty trail, and rushed on.

"Amanda!"

He shouted a few more times. She wouldn't turn.

The weirdest thing was she believed him now. With his black car and clothes, his mysterious demeanor, with those fucking sunglasses she wanted to tear off his face, she believed he was darkness. He was some sort of angel of death. Everything had been too weird to believe anything else. But why was the grim reaper helping her? To stop her from going to heaven? Or to stop her from dying?

When she scrambled the shrubs and got back up to the gas station, she cringed at the sight of his pitch-black car next to hers. She looked back. He was reaching out to stop her.

"Don't touch me! Just stay away from me!"

"Amanda. Stop."

She stopped at her car door. Then she put her head in her hands and cried. It was like she was suddenly crying over everything, from the near accident near Yuma, to being attacked near Mesa Verde, to the recent chase. She was marked, he had said. So she would die. And he was some evil demon helping her? John, her guardian angel, was telling her she was going to die soon.

She felt so confused.

"I have to go, John," she whimpered. "Please, don't touch me."

"Amanda."

"Stay away from me. Stop trying to help me."

"All right."

She looked up and squinted into his eyes. He had his shades off and this time, instead of lovely alluring blue, all she saw was his weariness. For a flash, she felt bad for him. It was almost enough for her to stop running.

She opened her door. He gently opened it wider for her.

"You're more than dark," Amanda said. "There's something sad about you."

"I can't believe I'm trying to stop you, Sherry. Yes, get away from me. Run home. Please. Run as fast as you can from me. Fly home, Sherry."

She slammed the door on him…but she didn't want to. And as she drove for miles alone, she already missed him. Yet she was too scared to look back.

Then she thought of his last words. He had called her Sherry.

*Who's Sherry?*

**13**

---

# PROTECT HER

"I didn't expect to see you back so soon," Sherry said. "What'll it be, John?"

John gazed at her through his shades. Sherry. Or an older Amanda? There she stood, with wrinkles and long silvery hair, leaning over the bar with an angelic smile. Once her hair had been blond, at least according to his dreams. With the same face as the girl he had just saved in Kansas.

John had seen nightmares. In his line of work, he'd witnessed bodies torn in half, bleeding, mutilated, burned, and knifed. He had lived a living hell. But never in this purgatory had he felt his world turn so upside down as when he stared at the older Amanda while thinking of the younger one.

"Just give me the whole fucking bottle."

"That bad, huh?"

John nodded. He looked behind him. The bar was quiet. There were only three couples sitting at tables under dim lights. The windows looking out at the parking lot were dark. Sherry put the bottle down on the counter before him. "Free of charge."

"No shit," he said, unscrewing it. Then he guzzled down the bottle. A quarter way down, Sherry touched his arm. "Easy. Don't you have to drive?"

"Of course I do. I always have to drive, don't I?"

"Tell me what happened."

He drank a little more first. Then he wiped his mouth with the sleeve of his leather jacket.

"She found out who I am."

"A hero?" Sherry opened her eyes wide and quickly put up a hand. "It's just a joke."

"Why are you so chipper anyway, Sher? I haven't seen you this happy in a long time."

"My friends and I are planning a trip to Arrowhead in a month for the summer. I'm just looking forward to it, that's all. Not that I like the mountains, but they thought I needed a change. So we'll be heading to LA for a few weeks for the mountains. Which means, sorry, but your psychiatrist will be out of the office. You'll have to see a real shrink or do without the therapy. Can you handle that?"

"As long as I have this." He pointed to the bottle. "I'm happy for you."

"Thanks."

John drank some more. Then he looked back at the place again. "When are you closing tonight?"

"Does it matter? So, what did you tell her? Please don't tell me you told her that demon shit."

"I am a devil," he said with a shrug. "It's a fact." He picked up the bottle. He didn't drink from it though. Sherry was right. He had to be ready in case Amanda was in trouble again.

*Why won't the girl just fly home?*

"Why'd you tell her that, John?" She folded her arms and shook her head. "You're an angel. I wish I could talk to the girl and explain. You're messing with her head."

"How am I messing with her head?"

"You're letting her into yours."

He chuckled and then drank some more over that.

"Listen," she said, leaning forward. She rubbed his arm. "You said you're happy for me. I'm happy for you. This girl is making you happy."

"She's driving me crazy."

"That's familiar," Sherry said with a shrug.

"I'm here to protect her. That's all. The minute she gets back home, I'll stop. Only Rick's still giving me jobs. I've failed for the first time. That damages my chances of ever getting out of here."

"Trap or not, doesn't your boss get what you're going through?"

"What's there to get?"

"You're in love."

"What!" John asked. He pulled his shades off and stared at her. Sherry didn't flinch. She just flashed him a rueful smile and slowly nodded.

"You're in love, John. What did you expect? You've met me at your age again."

John rubbed his whole face with his hand. He picked up the bottle and drank more than ever. Then he hit the bottle hard on the counter, pointing at her. "I love *you*. I've told you that for the past few years. You're the one who pushes me away."

"I love you too. But I also recognize when you love someone else. Be honest with yourself and this will be easier. When's the last time you left a job? Shit, even before when you lived with me?"

He turned from her. He heard her walk around the counter. She walked up to him and embraced him.

"I love you, Sher," John said quietly in her ear.

"I know."

"Then why would you say that?"

"That girl is me. You said it yourself. You said she acts

like me, looks like me, and has my voice." She stepped back. Then she ran her hand through his short hair. "You've gotta let *me* go. I don't mean the visiting—shit, I live for seeing you. I'll still be here. But you've gotta let me go *here*." She touched his chest. Then she sighed. "I understand. I've had decades to do this. You haven't, John." She touched his cheek and kissed his lips gently.

"We could try again," he said, looking down at the ground.

"It won't work," she said, shaking her head. "Take care of her like you would me. Guard her. Then love her like you once loved me. Not like now, like it once was for the two of us. Maybe this isn't a curse, John. Maybe it's a gift. Not from Lilith. Or Michael. Maybe it's a gift from God."

He took a deep breath and put on his shades.

"Whatever you decide, protect her. You're right to do that. The hell with Rick and the job."

## 14

# ROADSIDE MOTEL

The rest of the day had been unpleasant for Amanda. She had tried to enjoy the road, like she always did, but she couldn't stop looking over her shoulder. Nor could she regret leaving John the way she did.

By the time she had reached Kansas City, it was late. And she was hungry. She ate at the busiest restaurant that she could find downtown—because busy felt safe. Then when she arrived at her motel room, she didn't like it because it was too quiet and she was alone. She had never felt afraid to be alone before.

She washed her face and prepared to take a much-needed warm shower. She felt the water with her hand and it was, of course, cold. Then she gazed at herself in the bathroom mirror. Her long blond hair was shaggy like a bird's nest. And her eyes reminded her of John's. She had those same thick bags under them.

"I think this can be checked off as a fucked up vacation day, Mands," she said to herself. Then she dug in her pocket for her recorder to talk to her audience instead of herself.

"Well, guys… Caligirl's a bit deflated." She sighed. She

hesitated about what to say—which she never did—and then said, "Gettingold24 got into a car accident today. My green jewel still drives, but it has these huge dents along the side. It was pretty gnarly. But you know, it wasn't the car accident, it was the roads. That's what's still freaking me out. There was a car chase, police and all, in the middle of Kansas. Yeah, I'm not kidding. A car chase. And I was in the middle of it. This is all for real. And, well… I guess I'm still breathing. Sort of. So that's good. I'm still alive. Just freaked out."

She clicked the off button for a moment. Then she ran her hand through her long, messy hair. She replaced her recorder with a comb. She'd shower, cold or not.

She slipped off her flip-flops and turned the water back on. Then she removed her pants. But before she finished undressing, she picked up the recorder again.

"I lost my dark stranger. We had a fight, our second I suppose. Now the last. I don't know, I suppose it was cool enough to meet a stranger on a road trip. Right? And I mean, shit happens on road trips. Right? That's why they call it an adventure. It can't all be roses. Move on, Caligirl, move on.

"Should I just go home? Hmm. I'm over halfway to the Big Apple, but… I'm probably going to head back tomorrow. I'll let you guys know in the next entry. For now I'm signing off so I don't depress you any further. Tootles."

She removed her T-shirt.

That's when she heard a knock on the hotel room door. Who could that be? John? Would he have followed her? Of course he would. He was totally creepy like that. That's why, incredibly hot and attractive or not, she had run from him. But now she hated herself for feeling giddy that he was back. She quickly fastened the clasp on her bra and pulled on her T-shirt. It was a long enough shirt to cover her underwear. And she wouldn't open the door for him anyway.

*No way. Right?*

*Well…depends. Maybe he's brought roses or something.*

There was another knock. She laughed at her stupid joke.

"Shit," she said to herself, shaking her head.

*Should I even bother to answer the door? Why won't he just leave me alone.*

*Fuck him. I can take care of myself. I have fucking mace.*

She opened the door, but it was stopped by the chain.

"What!" Amanda cried. "Why don't you leave me the hell alone, John!"

There was a scream. It was her own voice. A figure was standing in the hallway with pitch-black clothes like John's, but it wasn't a man. It was a woman with long white hair and pink eyes, wearing a black leather jacket and white scarf over a motorcycle jumpsuit. There was another scream. From her own voice.

"Shut your hole and open the fucking door, Amanda."

"What do you want!"

"I want to talk to you," the lady said calmly. "Now open the door."

Amanda did the opposite. She threw her shoulder against it, but it didn't shut. Looking down she saw a boot in the crack of the door.

"Oww. That hurt. Unlatch the lock."

"Go away!"

"Calm the fuck down and undo the lock. I just want a word."

But she didn't. And the stranger didn't move her boot.

"What did he tell you?" she asked. "Did he say I want to kill you? If I'm an angel, why would I want to kill you, Amanda? If I'm good and he's bad, why do you listen to him? Did you ever think that maybe we're protecting you from *him*?"

Yeah. That's why she'd run from him. But she'd give anything for this woman to disappear and John to take her place right now.

"Go away!" She shoved her body against the door again.

"Oww! Fuck! If I wanted to kill you, Amanda, you'd already be dead. Now open the fucking door or I'll open it for you. I do breaking and entering for a living, and this is a goddamn chain lock."

"Help!" shouted Amanda. "Help!"

"Goddamn it," the woman said.

A white-gloved hand squeezed through the crack and ran a wire over the chain. The wire caught the chain and the door was pushed open. In a panic, Amanda launched her whole body at the door for a third time.

"You fucking bitch!" cried the woman as her foot was slammed.

Lilith threw the door open. Amanda fell on her back on the carpet. Her eyes bulged, staring at the motorcyclist now hovering over her. Then the woman shut the door behind her and, ironically, fastened the chain lock.

"Shut your dainty little cunt-voice," she said with a smirk. "'Kay?" She shook out her injured foot. "Just shut the fuck up."

The stranger was attractive but had pink, almost red eyes and pale skin. And the sight of her odd paleness made Amanda cry out again. Albino? Or one of these so-called pale angels? *Who knows anymore in this nightmare.* An assailant ready to rape or kill her? Yeah, that was more like it. Amanda quickly crawled backward toward the bed.

"Will you stop acting like a frightened little pussy?"

Amanda searched the room for something to strike her with. Her mace was in her bag.

She got up and ran for it, but before she could open her bag, her wrist was grabbed from behind. She was thrown against the bed. Amanda screamed again as Lilith twisted her arm hard. Then her other wrist was grabbed. Her wrists were quickly tied with rope. Then Amanda was thrown on the bed.

The woman let go of her and grabbed a desk chair.

"Let's talk," she said with a wicked smile. "Now you've been marked. And now you're bound because you're being an uncooperative little cunt. Calm the fuck down or all your fantasies of bad things will come true. Especially looking pretty and half naked as you are right now. I'd love to fuck that."

"Help!" Amanda cried again. "Help!"

"Shut up," the woman said, rolling her eyes. "Do I have to tape your mouth?"

Amanda shook her head.

"My name is Lilith. I am an archangel assigned by Samael to ascend you. I could have taken you in Arizona, had it not been for Azrael. We tried again on the road this afternoon. You know how that went."

"What do I—"

She raised a finger. "Don't talk unless I permit it or I'll tape your lips." Then she ran a finger along Amanda's bare arm. "It turns out, my lovely, that you arrived just in time. See, your friend is the best operative they've ever had. You're disabling him. That is more valuable than your ascension itself. For the first time, it's not really about you, angel. It's about him."

"What—"

She put her finger up again. "Shut up, Amanda, until I permit you to speak. I'm not done. Azrael and I have a long history together. Did he tell you?"

Amanda shook her head.

"You may speak," Lilith said with a smirk.

"He didn't tell me exactly what you guys were. He said angels, and then he just said I'm marked and I'm destined to die."

"Yes. That is so. You will die." She stroked Amanda's cheek with a white-gloved finger. Then she stared at her with her pink eyes. "My lovely, innocent girl, you will die. You're beautiful. Is that why he is breaking his pact? Or is he just tired?"

"I don't know about any of this." Then Amanda paused for a moment. Lilith was staring at her with this devilish sardonic smile. A grin that felt so evil, just as if the devil were here with her right now. "I don't know what's going on. I'm just driving a cross-country trip."

"Pretty, pretty," Lilith said. "Do you like my eyes?" She blinked them near Amanda's face.

"What?"

"Do you like my eyes? I was born with red eyes."

"Oh. I thought you—"

"Looked like all archangels?" Lilith asked with a laugh. She started going through Amanda's things. She even took out the mace bottle. She nodded and chuckled at that. "It's what Lilith looks like."

"It's nice."

Lilith nodded.

"What are you going to do with me?" Amanda asked.

"You mean?" she rummaged through Amanda's bag by the hotel desk. She looked at her compact and lipstick. "Am I going to have you ascend *now*?"

"Yeah."

"Not yet. You are his bait again. I told you..." She stopped going through Amanda's purse. "I was supposed to have you ascend in Arizona. Azrael saved you. Our spat earlier in the day was simply to prevent John from doing his job. You and he thought we lost. We didn't. The mission was a success. An angel died on his watch. And now, my dear, my hope is that capturing you will drive him completely crazy."

Lilith crossed her arms and just stared down at her. Then she walked across the room.

Amanda had to turn onto her side to watch her. She couldn't take her eyes off the woman. She was terrified of not seeing what she was up to.

Lilith went over to Amanda's spare bag and started rummaging through that too.

"What are you looking for?"

"Your goddamn phone."

"Why not just ask me?"

"I don't think you'll cooperate."

The phone wasn't in her bags. So she searched the room. It was lying on the counter near the TV. Lilith picked it up.

"What's the password, Amanda?"

"Why should I tell you?"

Lilith nodded and smirked. Then she walked around the bed. Amanda struggled to turn to her other side to watch her, but she couldn't turn fast enough. Then Lilith yanked her right hand from behind. "Let's see if you used your fingerprint." Lilith twisted her thumb and Amanda cried out in pain. She thought she was going to pull her finger off. Then she felt her phone against her thumb. Lilith grabbed another finger and bent it back hard.

"*Ow!*" Amanda heard herself whimper, but the bitch stopped bending it.

She couldn't cry. She couldn't appear weak. That's what this monster thought she was.

"You'll learn soon enough to not fight me," Lilith said, "or I'll just cause you more pain."

Amanda turned and saw Lilith scrolling through her phone.

"I don't believe it, you fuck him, but don't have his

phone number? Is it a code? Like it's this Jeffrey or Kurt guy? Or do you actually not have his phone number?"

"I never fucked him. I barely know him. He's as creepy as you are. Only he doesn't tie me up."

"I'm not so sure about *that*. Watch your mouth. When you say *fuck* it really turns me on. Especially when you add *tie*. You keep up your attitude and I'll do to you what he's been wanting to do to you all along."

"Are you gay?" Amanda cringed. Lilith's voice had been sultry and now she wanted to throw up.

"I love anyone, male or female, anything, my dear, if it leads to pleasure. Especially pretty little things." Lilith hurled the phone at her. "You're my worm. Don't squirm. If you move, little worm, I will cut you to pieces." She leaned forward so her face was an inch away from Amanda's. Then she grew a sinister, nasty smile. "If you resist, I'll fillet you like I did a nice Black woman a day ago in Idaho. Cooperate or suffer, lovely, pretty girl." She laughed— Amanda guessed it was over her disgusted expression. "Don't worry. You're too pure for my taste. You're simply bait, my dear. Simply bait."

**15**

---

# RETURN TO SANCTUARY

MULTICOLORED LIGHTS RUSHED PAST JOHN'S WINDSHIELD AS he drove at tremendous speed across the plains toward the desert. Slight turns of his steering wheel averted crashes. But obstacles were rare this early in the morning. It was daybreak. He was close to the border between California and Arizona. It was fairly empty and one of his favorite drives. But closer to California, it had dips. He slowed down for these.

It was when he reached fields of saguaros—shrouded in shadows by the freeway—that John really slowed. He whooshed by another trucker then dropped down to a hundred and fifty miles an hour.

Then he came to his favorite spot.

In desolation, he walked along a cliffside. His sanctuary. But it was still dark with only a thin line of light off on the horizon. He removed his shades waiting for the sunrise. It was far too early, so in darkness, he followed a path down an incline along an infinite desert vista.

*"What happens when you die?"*

It was his "aunt's" voice that came to him. His adopted mother.

"I don't know."

*"I think it gets brighter. The brightest light you've ever seen. Like staring at the sun. Then you're taken somewhere. Somewhere without pain. I fell once and hit my head. I remember such peace. It's when I woke up that I felt pain. I think it's like that. Tranquility away from our pain."*

"I hope so."

*"I hope I see your brother there."*

"You will."

*"Hold my hand, please."*

"I'm already holding it, Mother."

*"I'm scared. I'm scared."*

He scuffed the red sand against his boot. He felt dread. This memory was a mix of feelings. He so wanted to hear the voice of his aunt, but not this memory. Not this pain.

As if it obeyed him, he felt her presence leave him.

The first rays of light brightened the horizon. Below the cliff was a vista of orange and red over the weeds and saguaros. Empty sand for miles. He caught a large bird overhead circling in the dark clouds. It was reflecting the rising sun.

Amanda finally knew what he was. He was a monster. That's why she ran. Why was he so surprised?

So why did it still upset him? Was Sherry right?

His phone rang.

"Angel down," Rick said. "A man. Benjamin. He's thirty, Asian, bald, an engineer. He keeps to himself. His sign is Leo. He's traveling out in the open, leaving Minneapolis. You near there?"

"Not that far from there," John said, turning around and looking into the dark clouds toward Los Angeles. "A man?"

"A man."

"Send me the location."

"Are you back on board? We just lost another soul in

Florida because of your shit. I only have so many agents, Azrael. I've talked Michael into giving you this one last chance. But he said you'll pay for the two souls that passed."

He watched the bird circling above. Its shadow flew under the now dim stars. Right between the rising sun and the dark evening. That reminded him of himself. A wanderer in the shadows with just a glimpse of light. He remembered that, on her deathbed, his auntie had told him there'd be a bright light when he died. He yearned so much for that light now. He felt like Amanda had been a glimpse of it. The sun, even though it was blinding, was just a glimpse too. But he wore his shades to cover it all up…for the job.

"Send me the location," John repeated.

"I already have."

He nodded.

"John?"

"Yeah?"

"I'm going to tell you something as your friend. It goes against everything we do. But if I don't tell you, you'll never forgive me. Lilith's taken Amanda. She's getting off of Interstate Seventy near Columbia, Missouri, following her car. Intelligence says she stopped by the motel Amanda had checked into and now has her captive."

John gripped his free hand tightly. He pulled off his shades and stared at the rising sun.

"Send me her location."

"You need to go to the target in Minneapolis. Amanda is no longer your concern."

"I'm closer to Columbia, Missouri."

"John," Rick said, sounding uncharacteristically cautious, "listen to me carefully, man, for once in your life. Please. Listen. I just told you that we lost another soul. If you ignore the new target, this will make three failures. I might be able to work with Michael on the other two, but if I lose you this time and you do Lilith's bidding, your pact with us is broken. It's over between you and me and it's done for you. You'll essentially be viewed as working for them. We can't accept your attachment to someone they're using as a trap anymore… Damn it, John, is this one girl worth giving up your soul? You want to wander forever?"

John took a deep breath. It wasn't over indecision.

"Text me her location."

"This will be it between us. I'll send you two sets of coordinates. Follow the right one and I'll meet you back in Vegas tomorrow for a debriefing. Go for the wrong one and we're through."

"You would never have told me as a *friend* if you didn't know what I'm going to do."

"Then we're done. You're stranded. It's over. I'll be expecting your keys."

"And I'll meet you in hell, Raphael."

"Yeah? Try being careful around the police. Remember when we're through, you don't have my protection."

"Sure. And…thanks."

"Fuck off, John."

# 16

# CINCINNATI

Amanda felt more helpless than she'd ever felt in her life. Although she wasn't tied up and was allowed to drive —she wasn't quite sure why—the white-haired demon followed close behind, haughtily swerving back and forth, like when they pursued her in Kansas. If Amanda wanted a cup of coffee, the bitch followed her into the gas station. If she wanted to relieve herself, the devil was there too. She had almost escaped near a mall in Columbia, Missouri. It was of no use. The wily woman let her run; then as Amanda got back on the road, she was back to swerving pompously behind her car.

At a stoplight, Amanda had rolled down her window and asked her pursuer where they were going. "Just keep driving," Lilith had said.

Now Amanda had time to worry. And yawn. She was so tired after driving all night. And unlike in the beautiful open desert, leafless trees had sprouted up everywhere in Missouri. It wasn't as pretty.

Then it turned urban.

Amanda drove by the famous Arch—a landmark she

normally would be telling her listeners about. But she was hardly in the mood now. She slowed in traffic.

But soon traffic opened up, and they headed out of the city onto open roads again. And the demon signaled for her to keep driving.

It was the next city, Cincinnati, where she saw a black car streak past her on the other side of the highway. It traveled faster than any normal car. It had to be him! It just had to be. And before she could contemplate anything else, his sleek pitch-black car was nearly touching the back of Lilith's bike. Amanda felt safer now, until more black bikes appeared beside her car on the freeway. And there were more than ever before. Then she jumped as a few of them waved pistols at her and John.

Amanda slammed on the brakes and came to a stop, almost rear-ending a car in front of her. She hadn't been looking at the traffic up ahead. Then one of the pistol-waving bikers rode right alongside her driver's side window. He stopped and aimed the gun at her head. She ducked and screamed as glass came flying into the car.

*Again!?*

Amanda screamed. She sat crouched with her arms over her head, too afraid to sit up. Then she heard more metal crashing outside her now open window—and honking horns, and screams—this time from bystanders surrounding her.

Something was hurled into her car, hitting her leg. In the pandemonium she thought it was some kind of bomb. It hit the passenger floor mat. She bent down, but couldn't reach it.

"Amanda. Amanda."

She recognized that voice. It was John! Her guardian angel.

"Amanda!"

Somehow John's voice was inside her car. How?

"Get up. Sit up and hit the gas. Get the hell out of here! Now!"

She sat up. There was an opening in traffic in the right lane and she took it. Many cars were avoiding her. Why?

*Gunfire. They heard gunfire. Anyone hearing that would do anything to get away.*

"They're circling back," said John in a calmer voice. "Drive forward and stay to the right shoulder. Try to get off at the exit. I'm on my way behind you."

"John?"

"Yes."

"Where the hell are you?"

"I threw my cell phone in your car. I'm on speaker phone."

"Then how are you talking to me?"

"My car has another line."

Amanda's body was thrown forward and her head hit her steering wheel. Fortunately, she had a seat belt on and she didn't hit her head hard. It hurt though. From what? Most of the cars were staying as far from her as they could now. She glanced in her rearview mirror. It was one of the black bikes. But this guy wasn't brandishing a gun. Instead, he just kept ramming her rear bumper.

"One of them is right behind me."

"The right shoulder is open," John said. "Lose us. *All of us.* Lose us now. I don't think that dick has his gun. Hit the gas and run, Amanda!"

The guy was riding up to ram her yet again, but he missed. Because Amanda accelerated to the right as fast as she could just in time. She looked to her left and wished she hadn't. Lilith and three of her stooges were riding backward on the freeway near the center divider. Apparently, they had advanced between the cars ahead of them and were now circling back. And they were getting close.

The right lane blocked her again. But there was an off-ramp bridge leading off the freeway here.

"Take the exit now," John said.

"I can't. There's a line of cars in front of me."

"Drive on the shoulder again."

"What if I'm squeezed against the barrier and fall off the ramp!"

*I mean, what the fuck!*

"You don't have a choice," he said too calmly. "You have enough space. Trust me."

"How do you know? Where the fuck are you, anyway?" She leaned forward and searched ahead. Then she searched her rearview mirror. "I'm not innocent! Okay! I'm bad. Okay, John. Fuck, fuck, fuck. See! I cussed. *So get these fucking freaks off my tail!*"

"Lilith isn't after you," he said more calmly. "She's chasing me. She's using you to get to me. Take the shoulder. It's big enough for your car. I've scoped it out. If you drive fast and go, you'll make it."

She felt dizzy. Sick. But then she saw that bitch, Lilith, with her long, flowing white hair and scarf, only two car lengths from her side. It sure looked like she was chasing her. She was thrown forward again by a biker behind her. That was enough.

Amanda hit the gas and squeezed between the line of cars ahead of her and the rail of the highway to her right. The rail climbed more and more steeply, separating from the rest of the highway over a raised bridge. She was passing the bridge just like John had said she would. But then four, no all five, black bikes were right behind her. And the bikes had no problem squeezing between traffic either.

As the road started flattening, the shoulder became too narrow. She was forced to stop again.

She looked back through her rearview mirror. Then she jumped again. John's black car was airborne over an overpass. He must have launched off an adjacent freeway bridge. She thought he was going to collide with her car. He didn't. The black car landed short, crashing into her motorcycle pursuers. It smashed Lilith and another bike then rammed into a third, sending a fourth right over the off-ramp rail. Only one biker hadn't been hit. He stopped his bike behind her and rushed to Amanda's car.

John threw open his car door and tackled him.

Traffic moved again. That opened an exit.

Amanda did the same thing she had done on the bridge, quickly maneuvering around the cars surrounding her. After running a stoplight, and then another, she stared at her side mirror. Her pursuers were gone.

She was shocked to discover that she was alone in downtown Cincinnati. Then she looked down at John's cell phone. She reached down to grab it but jumped at the sound of a car horn. She was in the middle of a city street.

She drove another mile downtown until she found an indoor parking structure. She drove up to the next level, parked in a stall in darkness, and shut off her engine. The lot was lit only by slivers of daylight through a few holes in a concrete wall and a flickering light on the ceiling.

She heard panting. That was her breathing.

She looked down for John's phone, now in the shadows, but couldn't find it. It was too dark—and too eerily quiet. And John hadn't said anything since the freeway.

*Did they kill him?*

She looked at the passenger side mat. She couldn't see anything, so she turned on her cabin light. Dirt from another of Luane's cacti was all over the mat. And by the passenger door was John's phone. The screen was off.

She fumbled along the mat and picked it up.

"John?" she said quietly into the phone.

The screen was cracked too. But when she slid her finger over it, it lit up.

"John?"

The call hadn't been dropped. It was still ongoing. But there was only silence.

"John?" she said in a hushed whisper.

*Shit. Is he hurt? Dead?*

"John? John?"

## 17

## THE PARKING LOT

JOHN COULDN'T STOP HITTING THE BIKER'S FACE. EVEN after his foe fell unconscious, he kept slamming his bloody fist through the open visor into the guy's teeth. He heard yelling around him. Many people were sitting in their cars in traffic witnessing the fight. Some were shouting at him for wrecking their car with his crazed jump over traffic. Finally, he stopped bludgeoning the biker after noticing his own blood dripping from his fist.

He heard motorcycle engines. The other black riders were recovering. And they were weaving around cars, heading right his way.

"John," he heard through the car speakers as he jumped back in his car. "John. John." It was Amanda's voice. But she was talking almost in a whisper.

"Where are you, Amanda?" He closed the door.

"I don't know. It's…it's an indoor parking lot. Very dark. I thought they killed you. I'm so happy to hear your voice again."

"Where?"

"Where what?"

"Where are you?"

The minute John saw an opening in the traffic, he hit the gas. He got off the freeway and drove onto the city streets. Here the traffic thinned, and he was able to accelerate. He crossed two intersections. That's when he noticed silence in his car.

He wrapped his bloody right fist in a towel.

*Why isn't she talking?*

*She's scared. The fuckers blew open her window again.*

*I should have put a hole in his head.*

"Ditch your car, Amanda. I'll pick you up. You have your cell phone?"

"I can just use yours."

"No. Listen to me carefully. I'll text you the number to my car phone. Put that number in your cell and then call me the minute you get out of the parking lot. Then leave my phone in the car."

"What?"

"I'll text on the number to *my* phone. Copy it on yours and leave my phone in the car. Then get out of there."

"Why?"

They were right behind him. Five bikers with Lilith, the ringleader, in the center. As John felt a dip at the next cross-street, he watched all five of them drop down and jump a few feet up in the air. With all their visors down, he couldn't discern which biker was the man he had bludgeoned.

"What about my luggage?" Amanda asked.

"Leave your bag in the car with my phone. Hell, throw the phone in the bag. I can track the phone and we can get the car and your things later."

"I'm not leaving my belongings."

*Are you kidding me?* "I don't know how far you'll have to walk."

"I've got all my stuff in this bag," she said. "And it has rollers."

"We can get it later."

"No. I can't just leave it."

"Fine. Whatever. Take the bag."

"You don't have to sound upset."

"I'm not upset," he said with a sigh.

"I gotta tell you… I'd rather just stay put in this parking lot. It's dark and quiet. Why don't I just do that?"

"No. They'll find you."

"Okay, fine. I'll call you on my phone. Bye."

A block ahead was another line of cars. John steered sharply to the right, onto a quieter street. The bikers did the same. John passed a car, swerved around a pedestrian, and then hit the gas again.

That's when he heard a siren. A pair of police bikes with red and blue flashing lights rushed into the street, joining the chase. They were signaling for them to pull over.

John's phone rang. It was an unknown number—he figured Amanda's.

"John?" It was Amanda's voice.

"What are your cross streets?"

"Are those sirens? You got the cops after you?"

"Never mind. What's the cross streets? Quick. Get them for me."

She was breathing heavily. Then he heard the ding of an elevator door.

The road was blocked ahead. At the red light, he drifted right into oncoming traffic. He heard some horns. Then he swerved around two cars and continued down a narrower road.

John heard an explosion from behind. It was gunfire. The bikers were firing at the police. Another call came in on his phone.

"Amanda." No answer. "Amanda!"

John touched the dials on his console to put her on hold

and take the other call. The contact on the monitor read "Hunter."

"*I got a cop dead in downtown fucking Cincinnati, John!*" cried Rick on the line. "*Give me one reason, one good reason, to not blow you off the goddamn road!*"

"One?"

"Yeah."

"You owe me."

A bicyclist was in the middle of the street. John swerved to avoid hitting him. But the force of the near collision blew the guy off his bike. This was bad because John's pursuers were right behind him, and one of the bikers ran over him.

"I owe you?" Raphael said with a sigh. "Sure. Sure. This one time. You've got three minutes before we disable your car. This warning makes us even. I won't stop them from hitting you after that. And avoid pedestrians. I saw that."

John bent forward, looking at the sky through his windshield.

"Where are you?"

Rick hung up.

John quickly flipped through his console searching for recent numbers. He called the last one.

"Hi," she said. "I think I lost you in the elevator."

"Cross streets?"

"Oh… Hold on. Let me get past the gate."

John pressed another button and searched the map on his screen. She couldn't be that far away.

"Cross streets. Now, Amanda."

Lilith caught up to his car. She banged on the side window. Then two other bikes behind her crashed into his car. They were trying to push him off the road. They couldn't damage his car, but they could disable it by driving him into a building. John had to move faster.

He accelerated but then slammed on the brakes as two cars crossed the next intersection. A biker rear-ended him hard. That launched his motorcycle over John's car, and he collided headlong into another vehicle. John looked back. The biker's body lay on the ground motionless. Dead.

Lilith and the other bikers passed him. About a block ahead, Lilith was signaling for them to circle back.

John hit the gas and turned down a different street.

"Now would be a good time, Amanda."

In his rearview mirror, John caught a police bike being struck by a black bike. That made two police "disabled" and an innocent bystander killed.

"Amanda?"

Any minute, the entire police force of Cincinnati would be chasing him, and he wouldn't be able to save her.

"Cross streets. Now."

"It's Chestergate, John. Chestergate and… Dawn Street I think."

"I'll be there in a second."

He quickly typed in the address while swerving around a bus and a semi. There was a busy street with a red light ahead. He was right about being close. But he realized a big problem. Lilith was on his tail again with her stooges. If he stopped to pick up Amanda, they'd simply kill her while she was getting into the car.

"Amanda, how far are you from the entrance to the parking lot?"

"It's right here."

"Go back inside the structure. I'll meet you right at the entrance. You'll be safer in my car, but stay inside the structure till my car's there."

"They're still trailing you?"

"Yeah."

"I don't hear sirens anymore."

John looked at the digital clock on his dash. Raphael had said three minutes. He had about thirty seconds left.

"Are you there now?" John asked, staring at the parking garage.

"Yeah."

John slammed on the brakes. A bike collided with his car from behind. But Lilith evaded collision with the other biker by swerving in front of him. John hit the gas and accelerated toward the parking structure. He skidded right into the building, landing about twenty yards inside. Amanda was standing there with her luggage by her side staring with wide eyes.

John leaned forward and threw open the passenger door.

"Give me the bag." He reached for it. "Hurry!"

She handed it to him and he hurled it into the back seat. Then he tugged her arm, pulling her into his car.

"Close the door."

She was thrown back in her seat as soon as the door closed. John accelerated. The screech of his tires and his engine echoed inside the dimly lit parking garage.

Bikers were colliding with the passenger side. One biker hit the door. Then another goon took out his pistol and fired right at Amanda's face. She screamed, but the bullet didn't crack the window.

John looked in his rearview mirror. A line of red and blue lights were about to enter the lot. He couldn't exit the way he came.

"Put your seat belt on."

John floored the gas pedal. Lights flickered along the windshield. Then he felt the impact. He drove straight through a wall at over a hundred miles an hour. Fortunately, the wall was thin enough to penetrate and led to an outside road.

John turned right and sped toward a freeway entrance.

"I can't see!" exclaimed Amanda. "I can't see!"

"It's temporary."

"God, John, I can't see!"

"Just wait a minute. It'll pass."

John looked at his side-view mirror. A plume of smoke followed him as the wind brushed off dust from the shattered wall. The motorcycles were trailing him, but now they were caked with the dust from John's car.

His phone rang. The console read "Hunter" again.

"Look up, John. Your time's up."

John leaned forward. There was an orange helicopter in the sky.

"That's not ours," John said.

"No, that's a news chopper. You've been spotted. Find a spot and jump. Do it now. Get the hell out of there. And take that pale bitch and her bikers with you *away from the city* or she wins."

"You're not blowing me up?"

"Get the fuck out of the city before it's not up to me anymore."

He hung up on him.

Amanda was brushing tears from her eyes. Was she crying or was it the blinding light?

"The effect will fade, Amanda. I promise."

She nodded. But she kept rubbing her eyes.

John leaned forward to look up. He had lost the helicopter. For now.

Meanwhile, Lilith was pompously swaying back and forth on her bike with the rest of them right behind her. John found the entrance to the freeway. He drove on the shoulder.

"Are you all right?" he asked Amanda.

"You asshole!" she said, hitting his shoulder. "What is this about! How did we just drive through a wall!"

"I didn't know you saw it. Can you see now?"

"Yes," she said, turning away from him at the window. "But it burns."

"I'm sorry, Amanda."

"It's not your fault," she said with a sigh. "I know… Sorry."

"Do you have your sunglasses?"

"No. I left them in my car."

He checked his scope. He had an opening on the shoulder alongside a straightaway for at least fifteen miles.

"I need you to dip your head into your hands. Cover your eyes and don't look up until I tell you. We're going to jump, and it'll blind you again if you open them."

"I have to?"

"If we're to get them off our tail. Yes."

Amanda squinted at her side mirror. "Guess you saved me again. Thanks."

"Cover your eyes with your hands, Amanda. Do it now."

Amanda obeyed and crouched with her head in her hands. John pressed down hard on the accelerator. The lights rushed along the windshield. He and Amanda were thrown against their seats. She didn't scream this time. Nor did she cry. She didn't say a word.

John drove as fast as he could to lose the motorcyclists and escape Cincinnati. He could outrun them. He could lose them.

At first, they continued to chase him. But soon they fell back, not able to keep up with his car.

After an hour of driving in Kentucky, Amanda still didn't say a word. At first, John caught her staring out at the fields. Then she curled up like a ball, facing away from him, and fell asleep.

John watched her sleep for hours. Her chest gently rose and fell. Occasionally she'd shift a little in her seat, but she didn't wake up. Of course, that bitch had probably dragged her across the highway all night without letting her rest.

Why had he risked everything for her? She was beautiful. Sure. Pure and innocent. Good. Yes. She was an angel, yes. But John had known many beautiful women, many good women, angels, that had fallen. His boss was right. Amanda might look like Sherry, but she wasn't her. So why lose everything for her? Because she was special to him… Why?

*She's Sherry.*

A little later on, Amanda asked quietly, with her eyes still closed, "Where are we going, John?"

"East somewhere. Somewhere across the country. To New York, I suppose."

"Good. That's the last place I have to go to finish my trip."

## 18

# THE BIG APPLE

"D**ID YOU SEE THIS MIRROR**, J**OHN**!" A**MANDA CRIED**. "OMG, I can't believe it! It's like made of gold or something." John didn't answer. She really didn't expect him to. He didn't talk much.

They had checked into a hotel in Manhattan. It was the swankiest place she'd ever stayed in. There were these magnificent chandeliers by the entrance with vaulted ceilings, a large hallway, and an actual red carpet that led to grand elevators. It must have been over a hundred years old. And there was even an elevator operator with one of those cute bell-hop hats pressing the elevator buttons for guests. Amanda loved that. Now Amanda sat by the giant wall mirror fixing her long blond hair. It looked awful. It was frizzy again. And she still had bags under her eyes, like John always did.

She shrugged, removed her sandals, and enjoyed the feel of the swanky cool marble floor on her naked feet. They were filthy. She had thrown water over them in Kansas before she was kidnapped, but they were still dirty from when she ran from John yesterday. Yesterday seemed like a week ago—after driving all night.

She peeked through the crack in the door. She could just make out her guardian angel staring out the large hotel window—guarding them. From what? A bird? They were over thirty stories up.

"This place is amazing," she said.

He nodded, still staring outside.

"Whatcha doing?" She walked over. It was dark outside, but a thousand city lights twinkled from windows and the boulevard below. John was, of course, oddly still wearing his sunglasses.

"Lilith is still hunting you," he said darkly.

"By helicopter? Or does she walk on tightropes?"

He cocked his head, and there was a faint smile. "Why don't you get some sleep. My car was hardly a place to rest."

"I look that bad, huh?"

"No." He shook his head. "You look fine."

But then he was back to patrolling the window.

Amanda hopped on the bed. Then she pulled out her recorder from her pants pocket.

"Guys," Amanda said quietly, "I'm sitting on the thirty-fourth floor of a posh hotel before that dark stranger I was talking about. We're like two thousand feet up, and I feel like I'm in the fucking clouds. Can you believe that? It's a breathtaking view of downtown Manhattan. It's wonderful."

"Will you stop that?" John snapped.

"Shh." She said, gesturing for him to be quiet. She jumped up and stood by his side, looking at the ground. "The cars are just tiny lights from up here. And across the street, even in—like—the middle of the night, there are people walking along the sidewalk. But they're like ants. I mean, I'm on a top floor of an effing Manhattan penthouse. Can you believe that! And guess what that means? My mission to drive cross country is a success." She sighed.

"Yep, thanks to tall, dark, and handsome standing to my left." She laughed as he shook his head. She guessed he was probably rolling his eyes, but she couldn't tell through his shades. "They're like insects down there walking to God knows where. As I put my forehead on the glass and…look straight down, I'm imagining just floating in the clouds over all these people. Where are they going? What are they doing? I don't know. So many. Just another day for them in the city, I guess. Not for me. It's…exciting. Thrilling."

John shook his head again. That made her laugh.

"Yeah, my guardian angel is back with me," she said, laughing and falling back on the bed. "He's back. Freaky as hell, I tell you, but kinda funny. He's the kind of guy who doesn't realize he's funny. He's wearing sunglasses *in* our hotel room. *Inside* the room. I'm not kidding. I mean, who the hell even does that? He says he's an angel—a dark angel. Doomed to walk this earth damning people by saving their lives." John stared at her. "Would you like to say anything to my listeners, fallen angel?" She held the microphone of her handheld recorder up to him.

"Delete that."

"Let me tell you what happened," she said into the microphone, looking back at the window.

"I told you to stop it," John said. "You can't say all that to the public."

"'Kay." She clicked the recorder off and smirked at him.

"You can't say anything about me. Or what happened."
*Too late.*

He stared at her in disbelief. Then he slowly turned back to the window.

She clicked her recorder back on. "Back in Cincinnati, my car got abandoned in a parking lot somewhere in the middle of no-fucking-where. Then this guy drove me across Kentucky in his sleek man-car. My VW was totaled. I know, I'm in total bereavement over losing my green baby. But I think I can get her back. There were red and blue lights and sirens and all sorts of crazy shit in another car chase. I know you probably don't believe me, but truly, it happened. And, well, this guy and I got the hell out. I mean, guys, so many things have happened on this trip. You can't even make this shit up. It was fun, but scary as hell."

There was a knock at the door. Amanda looked up. John was standing right over her looking like he was ready to crush her recorder. Now he quickly gestured with a finger over his lips and signaled for Amanda to go to the other side of the room.

He rushed to the door. He looked through the peephole and then undid two locks. It was a maintenance woman handing him linens and a pillow for the sleeper sofa.

After she left, he went over to the couch and worked on putting together a makeshift bed, not saying a damn word. Amanda sat cross-legged on the bed just watching him.

*Boy, my guardian angel really has a stick up his ass.*

"You do realize your life is in danger?" he asked, tucking in a sheet.

"I don't need my bed that tight. I kinda roll all over the place."

"I'm not making the couch up for you. This is for me. You can take the bed."

"The fuck I will, John. I'm already blown away by this hotel. You realize that couch is probably more comfortable than a motel bed?"

"You're taking the bed. And I'd appreciate it if you stopped swearing so much."

"No. Fuck, no. I told you, I'm not an angel. And I'm also not taking the bed, mister."

He turned to her. His brow wrinkled under his shades. She smirked again.

"I don't really like how you push me around," she said. She surprised herself with how angry that sounded. "If my life's in danger, fine, I'll listen, if it saves my life. I get that. But if it's over bedsheets, I mean, come on, I say go to hell. Or…go back there…or something."

"Who are you?" he asked, still holding a sheet.

*Who the hell are you?*

He sighed deeply and said, "Sleep wherever you want, Amanda. Fine." Then, after fluffing a pillow and throwing it back on the couch, he returned to being a sentry.

"Well, I was about to shower when that pale bitch took me hostage. What I'd really like to do is shower."

"Why don't you go shower?" he said with a nod, not turning.

"I'd prefer it if you tell me the reason why you're staring outside. We're pretty high up. Does this Lilith have Spiderman's ability to scale walls?"

"If I spot their bikes on the road, it means she knows we're here."

"How can you see her that far down?"

He pointed to his shades.

"Hmm." She let out a big sigh. "I also don't appreciate being told what I can say to my fans."

"There are secrets that we're not allowed to share with the public. You can't tell them anything about me."

"But you can give those secrets to me?"

"You already know enough. And I owe you the truth. But we keep ourselves secret from the public, Amanda."

"I said you could call me Mandi."

"Your people can't handle the realization that you're being watched. Everyone thinks they act with free will. They don't realize, or want to know, that there are forces outside of your control.

"We unveiled ourselves centuries ago. It led to darkness. Plague. An end to civilization. What would be the motivation for human advancement with a realization that everything is out of your control? We learned from that, until today. If it means stopping me, I think Lilith will do whatever it takes. Even unveil us here in an urban center—the largest of them all."

"Well, since you're yapping now, how about telling me how we made it from Cincinnati to New York in a couple hours *by car?*"

*I mean, right? And, watch, he won't answer.*

"I have a fast car."

*See.*

She laughed. It wasn't out of mirth. "Do you realize how irritating you are? Not only do you not say anything, every answer to my questions leads to a few more." He didn't answer that, of course. "When will I be safe? That's the best one of all."

"After you get some sleep."

He removed his shades and rubbed his eyes. She enjoyed catching a glimpse of his lovely blues. It made her chuckle again.

"I'm glad you're in a good mood."

"Who said I'm in a good mood, John? I know what's happening. My car's totaled. I was shot at, nearly blinded. I'm in a hotel room in a strange city. With a strange man. And my apparent guardian angel tells me he's a devil and that I'm doomed to die soon. Doesn't that about sum it up? But, sorry, I don't brood. I just don't do that."

He nodded. Then he returned to searching the roads below.

"Why New York?" she asked. "I'm happy to complete my drive across country, sure, but why here? Why didn't you just return me to LA?"

"You need rest," he replied, not turning. "I told you, they hate the cities and LA was too far. I doubt they'll come here tonight. But we have to go straight home tomorrow."

"So maybe we should just hide here for weeks? That'd be fun. Just you…and I."

She smiled at him smugly as he finally turned. It was fun playing with him because he was so serious.

"I don't have weeks. I have to get back to work. We're heading back to LA tomorrow. I can get you back tomorrow after we rest."

He took a deep breath and went back to scanning the ground. He pressed something on his glasses. Perhaps he was zeroing in on something?

"John?"

He shifted his gaze in another direction

"John?"

"Yeah?"

She shook her head. "Who are you?"

He furrowed his brow over that one.

Then she reached for the TV controller. She turned on the television and switched to an old movie. Then a Dodgers game. She left it at that. It was an LA team, after all, and that reminded her of home.

"How long are you going to stand there?" she asked.

He just nodded, not even listening. She turned the television off, sighed, and jumped up from the bed again. Then she stood beside him and gazed out at the gorgeous view with him.

"This is much better than television," she said. "It's so pretty out there."

He nodded.

She was going to say more, but she faltered as he turned and gazed at her face. Even with those cursed shades, he was so handsome. His stubble was like him— ever so unkempt, like his thin dark hair, but perfect in its imperfection. She searched his face. "You really think you're bad? How many lives have you saved?"

"Hundreds."

"You're good," she said quietly, shaking her head.

"Mandi, when you die, I'll have another angel to damn. And then another. All to keep them suffering here on Earth." He turned back to the window. "I know I'm bad."

"You're good for me," she said in a hushed voice. She wasn't even sure if he heard her.

*You saved me.*

She found herself just gazing at their amazing view of the Manhattan skyline with him. She ran her fingers along his arm until she reached his hand. Then his fingers. She took his hand. He squeezed hers. Then she looked up at him. His profile. But he wouldn't turn. She reached up on her tippy-toes and kissed him on the cheek gently.

"Thank you," she breathed.

He nodded.

"John?"

"Yeah?"

"What're the chances you're going to find her down there? Even if she comes? Even with that gadget you're wearing?"

"What do you mean?"

"We're in Manhattan. There's millions of people downtown, even now at this time. I don't think you're guarding us. I think you're just trying to avoid me."

"What?" He quickly turned. Then he froze.

She giggled and stroked his fingers. Had she discovered his secret? He seemed uncomfortable enough to confirm it. Was that it? Was he just using his determination to defend them as a pretense to defend himself from his feelings for her?

He surprised her by embracing her tightly and leaning down and kissing her on the lips. They held each other before the window, kissing passionately. His hands drifted down to her waist. And he squeezed her closer. And they kept kissing. For the longest time. He didn't seem to care much about their defense now. Amanda wasn't even sure how long they kissed. But it was wonderful.

His hand touched her butt and she moaned. That embarrassed her. She moved back as he was still kissing her. Her face felt red hot.

"I… I think, John, I have to go shower."

He nodded, letting her go.

She laughed nervously and realized that, even outside his embrace, she still had his fingers in her hand. Seemingly a couple fingers at a time, he disengaged and she rushed to the bathroom.

She left the door ajar by a thin crack. Then she pulled down her shorts. She could see him, through the door, scrutinizing the city. And she knew that all he had to do was turn around to see her in her underwear.

"John? Have you seen this? I tell you, the bathroom is to-die-for."

*That is not the best choice of words, stupid.*

"I saw it," he muttered.

"I think…they used real gold. You should really check out the mirror. It's a nice view."

*Just cut it out and shower.*

But her heart was pounding. She watched him through the crack of the door. He turned and she saw his profile. He wore those shades and he kept pressing on them, looking in different directions. All he had to do was turn all the way around. But he was doing his job by the window again.

She pulled up her T-shirt. Then she unclasped her bra.

"You really should come here and see the marble floor. Come over."

"I already have."

She nodded and pulled down her panties. Then she felt her chest and face flush redder than ever at her embarrassment. She was naked before him. She stood there for a moment just waiting for him to turn.

"John? John?"

But he wouldn't turn. After waiting long enough, she gave a long sigh and walked into the shower. Of course the water was perfect. Hot. Welcoming. She hadn't showered in days.

She lifted her left arm and ran the bar of hotel soap along the curve of her breast and around her areola and nipple and, for a moment, she imagined he was washing her. Then she traced her body down to her waist, pressed her belly button, and cleaned her hips and waist—again, all the while imagining those strong hands she had just held. The hot water felt good and soon steamed up the bathroom mirror. She could see it through the clear shower curtain. No doubt he was still outside guarding her stupidly but in a romantic sort of way, because he was protecting her. She imagined him seeing her through the clear drape as she ran the water through her hair. It'd be foggy, but he'd see her profile clearly enough. All he had to do was turn. And he must have done that by now. Right?

She closed her eyes. She imagined him taking off his jacket and shirt, unveiling his ripped chest and abs, opening the curtain, and running those fingers through her long wet hair. She'd let him bathe her if he did that. Perhaps less erotically at first, soaping her back and her hair. But then the soap would flow over her ass and her private area. He'd orgasm her in the shower using the soap and water to lubricate his fingers. All the while he'd be making out with her again, kissing her just like he had at the window. Just as she imagined it, like heaven.

She was an angel, he had said. Innocent. Maybe she wouldn't be innocent anymore if he fucked her? And maybe that'd protect her.

*God, maybe you should make the water cold, Mandi. Won't you stop it!*

She reached down, took a dollop of conditioner in her palm, and ran it along her long hair. Then she cracked an eye open for a few stray glances at the door on the off chance that he was there. No luck. But the door was still ajar. Of course, he could hear her showering. All he had to do was turn.

Some of the conditioner dripped down the pale skin of her leg. She used the soap to brush it off her leg. Then she ran the bar up to her waist and toward the crack of her ass. Then along her pussy, washing there too.

She could walk out instead. Naked, hot, she could walk right out the door and just grab him. How could he resist? She knew from their kissing that he was attracted to her. And he was hardly innocent. What was his hesitation?

The water kept flowing over her naked body as she washed herself. As she kept just thinking of him. Thinking of his short hair and the stubble along his cheeks and chin. Now imagining his strong, hard body naked beside her, embracing her, then bringing her whole body against his naked skin. His cock now entering her.

She hadn't seen his skin, but she imagined his chest, from what she had seen in a T-shirt, to be rock hard. If he came in now, she'd run her hands along his strong muscles, his pecs and biceps. Then she'd touch his cock. She'd dip down on her knees and suck it while the warm water washed over them. Then she'd stand up and it'd be his turn to dip down. Then along her waist and over her pussy…

*Enough!*

She shut the water off. She wrung out her hair. Then she grabbed a towel.

She looked at her clothes draped over the vanity chair. She had forgotten to see if the hotel had a robe. And she had left most of her clothes in her luggage, still in his car.

So she patted her hair and body and wrapped the towel around her chest, covering a little of her naked body. For a second, she considered covering only her hair.

She opened the door wide. Her sentinel still stood there staring down at the street.

"I mean," Amanda said, "I suppose I can take the bed if you're gonna stay the whole night in front of the window."

John turned. He had his stupid shades on. But he couldn't hide his look at what draped her body—or lack thereof.

"Do you know if the hotel provides robes, John? Hmm?" She grimaced wide. It was all she could do to not laugh at his expression. And she felt her skin, already red from the hot shower, grow warmer.

"I can check," he mumbled. As he rushed over to a closet, she couldn't suppress a laugh anymore. It was funny to see such a confident man get all flustered.

He brought out an elegant white robe on a hanger and handed it to her. But she didn't take it. Instead she gently removed his sunglasses with both her hands. "Why do you wear this all the time?"

"Driving. You saw the light nearly blind you."

"But…you're not always driving? Not now."

"Always ready." With his naked blue eyes staring into hers, he seemed hypnotized by her. And she got lost too.

"Can I…have it?"

"What?… Oh." He handed her the robe. "Here."

"Lilith assumed we had…you know…done it. Why is that?"

"Archangels are dirty," he said with disgust. "Even my allies. Most of us view humans as objects. Especially Lilith. She's a demon."

"Yes, I think your enemies are demons. Not angels.

Whatever you say, John. You saved me. You didn't damn me by letting me live. I think that's ridiculous."

He nodded, but it was almost more of a shrug.

She embraced him again. She reached up and kissed him on the lips. "Thank you," she said quietly. "Thank you so much. You're my guardian angel."

Then they were back to it again, French kissing.

*I owe you my life.* She was not sure if she'd said that or thought it. If she'd said it, it had been between kisses. "But you seem…to be…repelled by me. Why is that, John?"

"I can't be repelled by you," he said, disengaging his lips for a moment. But she kissed him once more. "It's not possible."

"So, you find me attractive?"

Her towel fell from her body. No, it didn't fall. She dropped it intentionally. She was sure it was intentional, but he wasn't. He quickly reached down and grabbed it. Then he held it over her naked chest.

"It's okay," she said, kissing his lips again. "Forget it."

"No, it isn't."

"Why?" she whispered in his ear. "Why are you avoiding me?"

"I'm not."

She leaned her forehead on his chest and nodded. The towel was only covering her chest in front of him. He held her, but when his hand felt her back, it dropped over the wet crack of her ass. And his hand shook.

Nervous? How could a man with so much confidence be nervous around her?

"It's okay," she whispered in his ear.

"I'm not pure," he said.

"Neither am I," she said, this time pulling the towel away from her chest. She dropped the robe on the ground too. Then he looked down. Her breasts were pressed against his chest, and she entered his mouth with her tongue once more. "I'm not…happy…being pure… I'm only happy being with you."

They stopped kissing and John just stared at her chest. She felt herself blush again, but she didn't turn. She let him stare, his eyes drifting down to her legs. The light in the hotel was dim but seemed very bright with her nakedness. Then she helped him remove his leather jacket. And then his T-shirt, revealing his bare chest. Yes, his body was hard. And then…

Nothing was acquiesced. Nothing accepted. There was no contract of evil touching good, pure being soiled. No words. Only their hands touched each other. She let him stare again at her bare body. And she didn't blush anymore.

She helped him remove his jeans while he stared at her. It was as if he were taking a photograph of her to remember forever. She looked at his chest again—she had been right. He was well built. His muscles bulged. He was a warrior and his chest and abs showed it. She ran a finger along a scar. And then another. He had long scars along his arms and side. So many. Next his underwear came down. His legs and flanks were scarred too. She ran a finger along some of his scars, kissing along others. Then her fingers ran along the crack of his ass. All the while, they met each other's lips between glances at each other, now both naked in the dim hotel light. Finally Amanda tugged John's hand and led him to bed.

Amanda lay down on her back and John gently grabbed a pillow and put it under her head. He lay gently beside her. Then he leaned over, kissing her some more.

"If I am so good, John," Amanda said quietly between kisses, "take the good from me. Take me. Protect me from them. Make me bad. Make me impure and bad like you so they can't hurt me anymore. Make me be alive, like you… Fuck me. Fuck me now, John."

He pushed his cock inside her. At first, it hurt a little.

Then immense pleasure. A burning pleasure that only got better with every push. His weight beside her was enough to drive her wild. She pushed her pelvis back against him. Then her lips met his again.

"Oh, God, John you feel so good."

Faster. He started moving faster into her.

She turned to the window. It was unchanged. Still the twinkling lights of the city. There was darkness amid this light. Only the light from the bathroom allowed her to see the man she lay with. They looked deep into each other's eyes as he continued to push into her. His angel eyes.

He moved on top, his whole body now thrusting over her. She felt all his weight. He moaned, and that took her closer to ecstasy. He thrust faster. She had had oral sex before, but never penetration. And he continued to gaze at her with his angelic eyes. It had never been like this. She moaned harder, shaking in his arms.

He looked away as if they were done, but she moved him on his back. Then, on top of him now, she ran one hand through his short hair while the other moved his cock, rubbing it up and down. Then she dipped down and kissed him. Her hand brushed along the stubble of his cheek. He moaned again. She straddled him. Then she felt his cock move inside her again. He fondled her breasts as she bounced over him. She could hear their sex. The sound of smacking. It only made her bounce faster and harder.

John turned. This time he stared at the window too. To look for Lilith? Had he left his guard post? Or was it just the gorgeous view of the city?

She fell over him, grasping him so tight. He embraced her, almost hurting her. For so long, she had felt him pushing away. Now it felt like he clung to her, not ever wanting to lose her. And he was still inside her.

"I'm sorry," he said.

"I love you," she said, shaking her head. "I think… I

love you… Yes. I love you, John. Fuck me. Oh, fuck me, John!"

Even faster. She pressed her pelvis against him so hard.

He threw her on her back. And then he thrust again on top of her. Their lips met for a moment, and she felt him squeeze her body so close to his.

"I love you," he said.

"Oh, yes, John."

She climaxed again. Then she sort of collapsed to his side.

But now that they were done, he seemed unhappy. And in the light, he looked awkward. Confused. Had it been a mistake to desire him?

"Is something wrong?"

"No," he said, shaking his head. But then he turned his head from her.

"I guess… I'm sorry."

"It's not because of you, Sherry. I love you."

*Who in the hell is Sherry?*

**19**

---

# AFTER

After sleeping with her, she thought he'd open up. He didn't. He remained tight-lipped. In fact, he was back to being a sentry by the window. The whole night while she slept, he had been standing by that window. Maybe she was wrong about that? Maybe he really thought he could spot Lilith down below? She thought she might have seen him on the floor, leaning against the glass sleeping, at one point or even back on the bed, but by morning he was staring out the large window.

They grabbed coffee and food from a buffet at a restaurant. Then they were off early. She wasn't sure what the rush was, but John was very anxious to get back on the road.

Inside the car, she marveled again at his machine. The leather felt soft, almost like skin. It was a material she had never felt before. The black seats were ultra-comfortable, of course. The central console looked more like a cockpit with tons of multicolored lights. In the center was a computer that he constantly flipped through. It was primarily used to access a system of maps. But the maps seemed far more detailed than a normal navigation system.

He quickly merged onto the freeway. Even in early morning, they ran into traffic. The whole time, John scrutinized his side and rearview mirrors, just as he had done with the window at the hotel.

Amanda put her feet up on the dashboard and looked at him. He looked over and furrowed his brow.

"So?"

"So what?"

"I liked last night," she said.

"Last night was fun," he said with a nod.

"Can I give you a little bit of advice?"

"Sure."

"Smile." *I mean, he really has a stick up his ass, doesn't he?*

But he didn't smile like she wanted him to. That made her laugh. She was just teasing him.

He pulled out some sunglasses from the driver's side door and handed them to her.

"When did you get those?" she asked.

"When we were getting breakfast at the hotel. I need you to put them on. When the traffic clears, it's going to get blinding again. The effect will continue, but it will be bearable with sunglasses on. You still should close your eyes when the lights first appear. We'll be in LA in a few hours."

"A few hours? You're kidding me. It takes five hours to fly there."

"Five to drive in this car too."

"Hmm." She snatched the shades out of his hand. Then she laughed again. She didn't know why this time, she just did.

"You know, I didn't get to see Manhattan," she said. "We could have gone sightseeing. I've always wanted to see the Statue of Liberty. And the Empire State Building."

"There it is." And he actually pointed at the buildings off in the distance. "But right now, I need to get you home."

"'Kay… Can I ask you one more question?"

"Sure."

"What were you before you became a…well…a—"

"A devil?"

She laughed again.

"What's so funny?"

"You. You're so serious that you're funny. Yeah. A devil, if that's what my guardian angel wants to call himself. What were you before that?"

He didn't answer. That was okay because it gave her time to look out at the skyline receding from them. She leaned back in the passenger seat, pulled out her cell phone from her pants pocket, and took some snapshots. She had read about New York. She knew some of the buildings, like the Chrysler building. She couldn't see the Statue of Liberty. She saw a ton of bridges though. Along with a ton of cars.

"I was like you," he said finally. His response was so delayed that it took her a second to register what he was talking about. "I started out like you. Human."

"What'd my guardian angel do when he was human?"

"I'm not your guardian angel. Perhaps your guardian devil."

"Okay. What did my guardian devil do before he wandered the roads looking for pure angels to damn? And if you don't hurry with your responses, I warn you, John, I'm gonna bring out my recorder and ask you in front of my fans."

He turned and actually smiled at her. *Finally.*

"I was a cop."

"Well, that's predictable. You should have let me guess."

"I wasn't on duty all the time. When I wasn't on duty, I drove a car like this one. I was adopted. My aunt spoiled me. It was on a drive that I died, I think. Or my soul was taken between worlds and my new boss brought me back down to Earth."

"Did you have a girlfriend?"

He turned to her and she could just barely see him squinting through the shades. He was always acting like she was weird. And that was funny as hell too, considering what he was. In fact, she laughed in his face. She touched his forearm. She felt his strong muscle contract under his tanned skin from the touch of her fingers. Those same muscles she stroked last night.

"You don't have to answer."

And he didn't.

Then after a long silence. "Well, did you?"

"Yes."

"Oh, so you didn't just have sex with, like, every girl?"

"Why would you think that?"

"John, look at you."

"What about me? I had sex. Sure. But I fell in love with someone before I changed."

"What was her name?" Amanda asked, turning back to her window.

"Sherry."

*There's that name again… So that's who Sherry is.*

"That's… a nice name. What was she like?" Amanda put a hand out and John stiffened. "I mean you don't have to tell me…" She burst out laughing. She didn't know why, but being silly around this stiff board of a man was a lot of fun. And this time, he looked so serious.

"She grew old," he said gravely.

"There you go again," she said, rolling her eyes.

"There I go again with what?"

"What the hell does that mean? Your answers lead to more questions. What do you mean, she grew old? So? We all grow old."

"*Watch out!*"

John quickly passed between two cars. The move looked so dangerous that Amanda gasped, but he executed the maneuver as if he were simply passing a car. His car was only a few inches from the vehicle on Amanda's right.

"You nearly hit him!"

"Sorry," he said, looking at the side mirror. "When I turned into an angel, I was turned into an Azrael. Rick said the process of transferring one body from human to an angel takes decades. For immortals, time is insignificant. It wasn't for Sherry and me. After my transformation, Sherry had aged thirty years or more, while I was still the same age."

"I thought you told me you were twenty-eight?"

"In human years. But I lived in LA in the eighties at that age too."

"Okay, that's really weird."

He nodded. Then he pointed to an open road ahead. "When we merge, I'm phasing. That light's gonna come on again. I need you to keep your shades on. And you're not used to it. You might want to cover your eyes too."

"Sure."

"I'm sorry you're going through all of this, Amanda," he said with a sigh. "I really am."

"You can call me Mandi." Then she shrugged. "Remember? And I was looking for adventure."

John removed his shades for a moment and squinted at her. God, she loved that. Then he smiled. That was even better.

"Put your sunglasses on."

She fumbled with them. She noticed for the first time that her hands were shaking. And it wasn't just because she was in the presence of Mr. Handsome.

As the engine roared, she felt tremendous pressure pinning her into the seat. Light grew by the sides of the windshield. With shades, it was beautiful, like sparks of rainbows hitting the glass. Then the light spread, turning a bright white—as bright as the sun. She had to finally cover her eyes. John didn't. With his shades on, he stared right into it.

When they stopped accelerating but continued at a fast speed, it reminded her of being in an airplane. There wasn't much noise. It was mainly just his engine, which was probably quieter than a regular car.

"You all right?" he asked.

"Yeah."

"I'll have you home in a few hours, Mandi."

"Sure. Okay."

*Guess no more talking.*

But then…

"John, what did this Sherry girl look like? Was she pretty?"

He just stared at the road.

*Okay. No more talking, I guess.*

**20**

---

# GONE

It was around eight o'clock at night when Amanda was dropped off alone on a hill back home. She told John he wouldn't be able to park there, especially with his fancy car. It would stick out among the college apartments. So he had to just stop and drop her off. Of course he stopped it in the middle of the road, ran around, opened the passenger door for one last quick embrace (between some honking). And then said bye. And that was it.

Now a few students rode by her nearly knocking her and her rolling suitcase over. It was Friday and students from college were heading for parties. When she looked back, his dark car was gone.

*That's it. Gone forever. Well, Amanda, you wanted an adventure and he gave you one.*

Under a passing streetlight, she pulled out her recorder and pressed the record button. She wasn't in the mood, but she had promised herself she'd say something the minute she got back home. She tried to put on her best smile.

"Well guys, what can I say? Trip's done. The whole thing was amazing. I saw spectacular open desert roads. I saw Denver, Pittsburgh, Phoenix, Cincinnati, and New

York City. For a journalist like myself, I just had to see the country. And I did. I wouldn't have had it any other way. Even with all the danger."

She clicked the stop button. Then she ran across the busy street. She looked back at where John had dropped her off. Yeah, he was gone.

In darkness on the sidewalk, as she walked up the rest of the incline, she clicked her recorder on again. "They say that going on a trip across the country alone is dangerous. Sure it is. But it's something you guys should all do."

She nodded over that and clicked the stop button. She wouldn't tell them about John anymore. Of course, those who listened would wonder. But she had promised him she'd keep mum and even edit some of the angel stuff later. She'd keep the Denver interview on the top of the museum, though. That was just way too good.

She jingled her keys and opened the door. It smelled like tomato sauce. Luane was probably cooking. Seeing Lu was the only thing moving her legs now. But when she crossed the threshold, the apartment was empty. The lights were on, but it was way too quiet. She walked into her living room. Then she meandered over to the bedroom. "Lu?" And then the other bedroom. Empty.

Then Amanda felt sick. Dishes and food were strewn on the tile floor of the kitchen. The tomato smell was from spilled spaghetti. On the counter by the mess was a note.

*"My dear fallen angel, we failed at taking your soul. He sullied you. So we shall now go for another. If you and Azrael want to ever see your roommate again, meet me and Samael in Bakersfield. There Azrael can have sanctuary and discuss payment. But he cannot go alone. I request the presence of you, Amanda. Azrael cannot go alone if you ever want to see your friend Luane again.*

*Everlastingly yours,*

*Lilith."*

Amanda felt short of breath. She felt like the air weighed heavily on her. Then she felt sick.

She ran to the bathroom and threw up in the toilet. As hard as it all had been—through car chases and a kidnapping—there was nothing worse than this, nothing worse than worrying that something would happen to her friend. And this was her best friend.

"John!" she shouted. "John!"

She ran back to her purse and rummaged for her phone. She looked for his number but couldn't find his contact on the list. Then she checked recent calls. There were no new numbers. Had he erased it?

*That asshole!*

She remembered he had told her they would never see each other again.

"John! John!"

**21**

---

# SHERRY'S

"I'm sorry, John," Sherry said with a rueful smile, leaning over the bar and touching his arm. "I'm so sorry."

Angel Dive was busy. It was Friday night, but Sherry had help and after seeing him walk in, being sensitive as always, she seemed to know something was wrong. She led John to the end of the bar, where they could talk. Now he felt like he was spilling too much of his problems, along with his whiskey.

"Life is unfair," Sherry added.

"This isn't life," John said with a nod. "Leaving her, I felt like I was losing you."

That seemed to upset Sherry. A lot. She looked away.

"Now *I'm* sorry," John said, touching her arm.

Sherry flashed him a fake grin. "How is the young girl holding up?"

"I practically threw her out of my car. But she understood. I'm not good at goodbyes, as you well know. And having her hang with me longer only would have been more painful."

John drank down another shot glass. Then he tapped a finger for another. Sherry shook her head.

"Why don't you stay sober tonight, John," Sherry suggested. "Stay with me tonight. You know, Rick could need you any minute. Or the girl could still be in trouble."

"I sullied her."

"God, John," she said putting a hand up, "I don't want to fucking hear about that."

"Then don't," he said with a nod. "But…" He removed his shades and looked down at his glass. He tapped the glass again.

She rolled her eyes and went behind her counter, grabbing a bottle. Then she poured him more whiskey. Someone asked for her help but she ignored him. Then she walked back and leaned over the counter.

"She really looks like me? Seriously?"

"Samael and Lilith did their homework," John said with a nod. Then he reached across the counter and touched Sherry's cheek. Wrinkles and all, Sherry was the most beautiful woman he had ever known. So was Amanda…

Sherry pulled back and shook her head. "Life goes on. As long as you're here, move on."

"I'm here."

John's phone rang. The bar was a bit busy, so he got even closer to the wall to hear. The contact read "Hunter."

"We're still talking?" John asked.

"Angel down. Luane." It was Rick, but he wasn't sounding like his usual self. Instead of sounding characteristically indifferent, now he sounded grave. "Luane is twenty-two, Asian, long dark hair, just graduated an English major, looking for a job in journalism. Born a Virgo. She's rooming in an apartment with a girl named Amanda in Santa Monica. Amanda. *Your* Amanda, John. This is Amanda's best friend and roommate." Raphael dispensed with his usual banter, but the silence was worse. For a moment, John wondered if his boss had hung up. He heard laughter across the bar amid all the talking. "I'm sorry, John. It's her friend. You finally did everything right getting the girl home, but—"

"Where?" he snapped. "Did they get her yet?"

"They have her. Lilith wants to talk to you privately for an exchange. She's asking for sanctuary. She probably wants to speak with you to turn you. Then maybe she'll give back the girl. But you know how this works. She'll offer anything you want, I'm sure. You know the price. But the girl dies if you don't go."

"I'll fucking talk to her. Where is she? Send me the location."

"Listen, John, you know as well as I do that Luane's days are numbered now. This isn't about snaring you. You saved Amanda. This is payback. Most likely, they will kill the girl, if they haven't already. Let Luane go and forget this. Don't get caught up—"

"You really should stop fucking trying to convince me not to do something you know very well I'm going to do."

"I'm your friend." There was silence. "Amanda won't understand any of this, you know. If you see her again, you're going to give that girl false hope."

"Then I won't see her."

"You have to. They've requested her presence with you in sanctuary or they will kill Luane."

"Text me the location," John said.

"Where are you at?"

"Sherry's."

"Give her my regards."

"Fuck you and text me the location."

"Already done."

"I'm doing a job this time. Can you help?"

"I think so. But I'm far south—outside the United States, near Mexico City. If you're in Arizona, it's gonna take you a lot less time than me."

"Where did they take her? What city?"

"Bakersfield."

"I'll see you in Bakersfield."

"Sure, John. Sure."

John hung up the phone.

"What's wrong?" asked Sherry. He hadn't realized till now that she was watching him.

"They took her best friend."

"Oh, God. This has to end!"

"Goodbye. And thanks, Sher." He jumped up and headed to the door.

"Hey, John. Be careful… I love you."

## 22

## BACK IN LA

AMANDA SAT ON HER COUCH WITH ALL THE LIGHTS TURNED off, in the middle of the night, just staring at a wall. She didn't know what to do. Her car was still in Cincinnati. Her best friend's car was missing. She was desperate for help, but that bitch Lilith hadn't even told her where to find her. Bakersfield? Where? And John…how could he just leave her without his number?

*'Cause he thinks he's a devil.*

The nut. That sorrowful shadowy sullen nutjob.

Oh, what she'd do to see him now.

God, she was so worried about Lu. And now it was the middle of the night. And it still smelled like old spaghetti. She hadn't bothered to clean up the mess in the kitchen.

She could rent a car? Tomorrow morning. Nothing was open now.

There was a knock at the door. Amanda rushed over, nearly tripping on herself, and unlocked and threw open the door.

"Don't you look through your peephole?" John asked.

"Where were you!" Amanda hit his chest a few times with her fists. "How could you leave me home and erase your number! You're such an asshole! I told you not to do that! Didn't you think maybe I'd still be in trouble?"

"We have to go now, Mandi."

"What? Now? Really? Oh… I know. I know. But…it took you long enough!"

She ran over to a table in the dark and grabbed her purse. She hadn't even changed. She was still wearing the same T-shirt and jeans as when they left the hotel in New York. John hadn't changed either. He probably never changed, for that matter. He had on the same leather jacket, black shirt, and black pants. And shades, of course, even though it was dark outside. But he smelled good. He always wore fresh cologne.

Before Amanda knew it, he was running, dragging her behind him, to his super car. They hadn't said another word. He hadn't even objected to being hit in the chest, though she didn't hit him that hard.

"Sorry," Amanda said.

"For what?"

"For hitting you."

He laughed. Then he looked across the street. Seeing his super car across the street in a neighborhood of apartment-dwelling college students with their cheap cars was pretty weird. It was parked in front of a driveway. There was no other spot on the street even at this hour.

"At least I can still make you laugh."

"Yes, Amanda."

"I need your phone number again. And don't you dare erase it. You know, since I met you weird things keep happening—like a crazed demon-bitch friend of yours kidnapping my friends. It would have been nice to have your phone number, John. I need it and you're not going to say no."

"All right."

"Right."

She loved it when he opened the passenger door for her. But she held his arm before he closed the door. "Your phone number. What is it?"

"Now's hardly the time."

"I won't let you go and we can't save my friend until you give it to me. What is it? Now that we know each other better. And…you…you know—last night." She pulled him to her and kissed him on the lips. "Give it to me. Give it to me now."

He reached for her phone. Then he went to contacts and typed in a number. He handed it back to her.

"Lilith said you dirtied me. She wrote the word *sullied*."

"I did."

"Thanks for doing that." She put an arm around his neck and clung to him by the passenger door. "I'm scared, John. Will you do everything to help save my friend?"

"Yes."

But she didn't let go of him. "Promise."

"I promise. We have to go."

**23**

---

## THE TALK

"WE NEED TO TALK," JOHN SAID.

*That's a first.*

She turned to him. They were both wearing sunglasses. They were moving at an incredible speed down the highway with shadowed hills and valleys rushing past the windows, and they could because the roads were clear and it was the middle of the night. Red, green, yellow, and blue lights bounced along the edges of the windshield and the side windows like rain.

"John, you never say a thing."

"I need to now," he said sternly with a nod. "There's a lot riding on this. Lilith might be with Samael this time."

"Who's Samuel?"

"Not Samuel. *Sam-a-el.* Samael is the devil. It's an ancient name. He's also known as Satan."

"Oh," she said with a nod. "That Samael."

She looked out the passenger window. She thought she was in the desert, but she could barely tell, it was so dark. Ever so often, a building would speed past. And John frequently inched the steering wheel in different directions, quickly passing cars and trucks on the road.

He laughed.

"There's another first," Amanda said. "You're laughing. I don't think seeing Satan is very funny, John. Can you do me a favor? Just lay it on me. Tell me everything. When you feed me a little surprise here and there, you freak me out more."

"I laughed because you went silent."

"So Satan and Lilith are meeting us in Bakersfield? Great. I don't know. Yeah, it sounds kind of funny in a twisted way. Are there any good angels, aside from you, John, that will be there too?"

"I'm not good."

"Let's not go through that again."

He was so focused on the road. The landscape was whizzing by. She touched his arm. "Now you're claiming Satan is here to help bring the innocent to heaven? And what about Luane? John, I might have been a virgin before I met you, but Lu absolutely, most definitely, is not virginal. She's a certifiable liar, gluttonous, envious, and a cheat. That's why I love her so much. She's fun. I really think you guys aren't playing by the right rules. Your demons are good and your enemies are angels. But you insist that you're fallen and damned. Look, even when you were out protecting me, I wasn't *that* pure."

"Amanda," he said, quickly shaking his head. He turned to gaze at her. "It doesn't matter. I have to warn you. Your friend's in grave danger. I'm not sure I can save her."

"I'm always in grave danger around you. And you saved *me*."

"They won. By delaying me, she turned you. And while I helped you, she killed another two souls. Now there's no reason for them to keep Luane alive."

"We have to try." She glanced at the road again and nodded. Her nod was more to herself.

The shadows of mountains rushed by her like buildings do on the freeway. And those weird colored sparks occasionally scattered around the passenger window. She didn't dare look at the speedometer. At last glance it was over four hundred miles per hour.

*Oh, Lu, I'm so worried. We just have to try. It's my fault. I should have just let these freaks kill me.*

"We have to do everything we can," she said. "Do you hear me? Everything, John."

"I will."

She turned to the window again. She felt tired.

"Where are we?" she asked.

"Near Grapevine. We'll be there in a few minutes."

"What's this "sanctuary" thing mean? Lilith wrote that in the note. What does "sanctuary" mean? Are we meeting in a temple or something?"

"Sanctuary is a pact. It means both sides, good and bad, have agreed to come together and not fight. It's how we make agreements. If she keeps to her word and holds sanctuary, then your friend will be safe. Until sanctuary ends."

"And when do you agree for it to begin or end?"

He looked in the rearview mirror. Then he effortlessly passed a group of cars by driving onto the shoulder.

"When it's mutually agreed."

"So…have we agreed?"

"Not until we talk."

"And is that possible?"

"What?" he asked, turning to her.

"Talking? You don't ever talk."

"Yeah."

"I've made a decision," she said with a sigh. Then she kicked her feet onto the dashboard and scooted back again.

"What's that?"

"This isn't just about Lu. You're never leaving me ever again, mister. Do you hear me? Never."

He looked at her. She gave him a big grimace and chuckled. He didn't smile. He just stared back at the road.

**24**

---

## BAKERSFIELD

THE YELLOW AND RED RISING SUN WAS BREATHTAKING AS always for Amanda. It had first shown its majestic beauty rising slowly above a dark hill. Then after they had wound down a valley, it had reappeared along a long stretch of highway. She could see empty land for miles now. Still, few cars were on the road this early in the morning.

Amanda knew they were entering Bakersfield as they whooshed under an overpass. Indeed, they would be there in minutes. Amanda couldn't believe how fast they'd gotten there. Then the car decelerated and the color splashing on the windshield ceased. John touched his central monitor and dragged his finger across maps, shuffling through them.

A bird soared above the car. It seemed to be following them. She watched it through her shades as it passed over the car. The bird was so beautiful, so majestic. It wasn't all that different from John. No home. Their only purpose was seemingly to hunt.

"They're not moving," John said. "They're waiting for us."

For a moment, she caught red and blue flashing lights.

John glanced at his side mirror, but then returned to checking his monitor. The digital speedometer still read one hundred and seventy five.

"We're slowing down to normal speeds."

"Thank god," she said. "What about the cop?"

"We've already lost him."

The sun rose and she could see buildings as they approached the city. And even this early, traffic was thickening. John was swerving around more cars.

"You okay?" he asked.

"Just a little car sick. And…no. I'm not okay. I'm worried."

"I can slow down more."

"For Lu, no. Don't slow down."

He nodded.

"Why do you keep staring at that map?"

"I'm calibrating their location. But…it's strange. I was tracking them. Now, if this is right, we should be driving right up their ass."

"How can you see it in the dark, anyway? It's so dim." She removed her sunglasses and pointed to them.

"Special lenses," he said, turning to her. "I can see you too."

Then he was back to his map vigil.

"How do you get all this stuff?"

"Hmm? What stuff?"

"The car. What is this machine anyway?"

"It's an old car."

She laughed and rolled her eyes. "There you go again."

"It is. It's an adapted GT40. I had one in my past life. This is military grade. CIA stuff." He was still counting. "We get this from the government."

"The government supports devils?"

He nodded. Well, that wasn't so hard to understand.

"I don't know all the odds and ends, really. Don't really

care, Amanda." He started mouthing what seemed like numbers.

"Why are you counting?"

"I'm figuring out their exact location from these coordinates. It's about thirty more seconds."

The rising sun shone over a bridge about a mile ahead. Whereas before, they would have already passed it, traffic was slowing them down. That's when Amanda saw them. On the bridge were a motorcycle and two people.

"Oh my God, look!" Amanda said. "There she is!"

John looked up from his monitor.

It was Luane, her hands tied behind her back. And it looked like her mouth was covered with tape. She was wearing just a white T-shirt and shorts. The person beside her was in a black leather motorcycle jumpsuit, and long white hair trailed from her helmet.

"Oh no," she said.

The words came out of her mouth almost before the sight registered in her brain.

*Crack.*

It was so loud that it almost sounded like it came from inside the car. Luane's body fell on the sidewalk of the bridge.

Amanda heard a scream. It was from a nearby car. Or was it her?

*"Lu! Lu! Oh my God!"*

Light filled the car as Amanda was thrown back in her seat. She clutched her head as her eyes burned in pain. She was blinded again. Then she heard some grunts from John. It was gibberish. She looked and, after her eyes burned, she saw only a shadow of him. He had done it again. He had launched his car after she had taken her sunglasses off.

Then as quickly as she fell back in her seat, she was launched forward. The seat belt hurt her shoulder and chest as it stopped her from being thrown into the dashboard. The force was so hard that the belt dug into her skin. She was pushed against the car door. She worried that the force would throw her out. She was pushed violently back against the seat again. Then she was thrown forward once more.

The car screeched to a halt.

John's seat belt clicked. Then his shadow reached over her. He was opening the glove compartment. He pulled out a bag and threw open his door. Then she heard gunfire. The noise mixed with her burning eyes was horrible. She covered her whole head.

Then she thought of Luane.

*Oh my God! Lu!*

The realization was cloudy in her mind. Between the constant explosions from John's gun and her blind eyes, she didn't know what was happening. She was trying to accept the fact that she had just witnessed the execution of her friend. But she still couldn't even see.

The driver's side door slammed shut.

*I can't see! Damn it, I can't see!*

*I have to see. I have to see if Luane's all right!*

*How can she be all right? She was shot in the head.*

The pistol fire continued. It wasn't just John. There was another gun firing further off. They were in a shoot-out. A stray bullet ricocheted off the windshield. And a shadow of a man ran toward a motorcycle on the empty bridge. She could only see John's halo of light in the darkness. Her guardian. Her angel. He was brazenly rushing toward the motorcycle, holding his pistol with two hands, firing like crazy. He'd run out of ammo and reloaded from the bag he was carrying. And then he was firing again. He didn't even bother to seek cover.

As her eyes adjusted, she saw Lilith firing back behind a bullet-ridden parked car. A few stray bullets bounced off the windshield driver's side window again. Amanda could now make out the features of the motorcyclist. It was Lilith with her stupid white scarf for sure. But John was firing so crazily that she couldn't safely get back to her bike. She tried a few times, but it looked like the demon was limping. He must have hit her.

Finally, the bitch managed to hobble to her motorcycle. She got on, spun around a bit on the now empty bridge, and sped off.

John sprinted back to the car. He paused for a moment looking at the opposite side of the bridge. Before Amanda could turn, she heard them. She saw red and blue flashing lights approaching their car behind them.

John swung open the door. "Get out, Amanda! You'll be safe in the police's custody. Get out. Now!"

She shook her head.

"I'm chasing her!" He pulled his shades off and stared into her eyes. She looked into his blues. They weren't sweet now. His eyes were bulging. His tanned skin had reddened. "Get out of the car now!"

"She's already dead, John. Forget it."

His mouth clenched. "I can go after her. I can get back at her. Now get the fuck out of my car!"

Amanda stepped out. John jumped into the driver's seat. He hit the gas so fast that she hadn't even completely closed the door. It shut after the car flew forward. She watched his car shimmy and drift across the bridge and drive toward the motorcycle. Then it went at an unnatural speed, disappearing in the distance like a black blur.

A body still lay on the empty bridge.

Luane.

*Oh, God.*

Amanda ran across the bridge but halted at the sound of two approaching squad cars.

"Put your hands up!" she heard from a megaphone. "Put your hands up now!"

She raised her hands. She stood like that for what seemed like forever. Then some force, at first she thought it was wind, knocked her down. An officer had tackled her. She got up on her knees and saw a red flash of light. It came so close that she and the man who had apprehended her were thrown back on the asphalt. This red car, similar to John's black one, sped after John and Lilith.

Soon a whole squad of police cars filled the bridge.

Amanda looked at Luane. Her vision was still blurry, but she could see her friend clearly enough, lying motionless. Lu's eyes were closed. There was blood beside her head on the sidewalk.

Someone lifted Amanda from behind. Her arms were yanked back, and she felt metal handcuffs.

"You have the right to—"

"*Go help her!*" Amanda shouted.

**25**

---

# STILL GREEN?

IT DIDN'T TAKE LONG FOR JOHN TO CATCH UP TO THE motorcycle. That didn't surprise him. They were maneuverable, but his car was faster. But the red streak behind him was a surprise. His phone rang through his speakers. The contact on his monitor read "Hunter."

John answered it.

"Don't do anything stupid," Rick said.

"I was told I was going to meet Lilith and Samael in sanctuary," John said. "They asked me—"

"I know. I know. I know the whole thing, John."

"I'm not done. They asked me to bring Amanda. They then proceeded to knock off her best friend execution style, in broad daylight, on a highway bridge in front of us. They brought Amanda to watch. She was already sullied, according to the bitch, by me. Why did they ask her to be there, Rick? What was the point?"

"You're talking about Lilith, John."

John took a deep breath. He looked out his window. He rarely drove this fast, especially during the day. The multicolored lights were splashing against the sides of his car, and he was thrusting up hills and back down like a rocket, so fast that he felt airborne a few times. But he was closing in on the bike.

"Azrael—"

"Don't fucking call me Azrael! Don't ever call me Azrael again. I'm done. I played by your rules. I saved your lives. Now it's clear that we've done things all wrong. We should have gone after the people killing the angels all along." He looked at his console thinking his boss had hung up. There was silence. "Clear the road," John added. "I'm going to do everything I can for justice. Maybe I'll shoot her in the head too. Clear the road."

"I think you're running out of bullets. And it wouldn't do any good anyway."

"Then I'll run over her."

"You can do that. Okay. You can do that, John. But what's going to happen to you after?"

"Why'd she do that to Amanda?"

"She's Lilith."

"What's her game?"

"Look what it's doing to you. Just like Vegas, she's confusing you and—"

"It ends this morning."

"You've nearly run over two cars since I've been chasing you. You're driving too fast and about ready to kill innocent people downtown."

"*She's* driving fast! I'm following her. Do the rules about killing the innocent not apply to her?"

"I have drone footage showing that you shot her in the chest while she was off the bike. She's hurt. She'll likely die. Stop the chase now. Let her go," Raphael said with a sigh. "Please, man. You've done enough."

"Was Samael there?"

"No. He's in Mexico. That's why I was down South."

"Of course. That was a lie too. I'm going to end this now."

"John," Raphael said sternly and slowly, "listen to me very carefully. This isn't going to *ever* end. You can't kill Lilith. Or Samael. Another devil will take their place. Just like if they kill you, there'll be another soul replacing Azrael. It's about saving lives when people need us. It's about your soul's salvation. You can't change the system."

"Lilith just executed Amanda's friend on a bridge in front of her eyes. And for no reason other than to fuck with her head. Was that part of your system? *Now clear the fucking road!*"

He was passing Valencia into Los Angeles. They had traveled hundreds of miles in minutes. Now traffic was getting thick.

"She's driving you into the city. You might want to kill her, but she's goading you. She still wants you terminated, and getting you angry is her plan. You asked me why she did what she did, this is it. You kill her, she'll kill you. You have no backing from us in the city. Drop the chase now."

"Clear the road."

"Oh, for fuck's sake! I can't clear all the police from downtown Los Angeles! If they see your car speeding, they'll go after you. Turn your car around or we'll stop you. Do you understand? We'll stop you. Friend or—"

John hung up on him.

Lilith was swerving left and right, merging between cars, taunting him. If she was hurt, she hardly showed it. As the traffic got heavier, she showed him the middle finger as she squeezed between more vehicles.

John drove to the right shoulder and hit the gas. Traffic rushed by him to his left. One car was turning into the outside lane, and John rammed right into him, spinning his car into the stop-and-go traffic. It wouldn't damage his car, but it would make everyone notice him now—including the police. Of course, Rick was right. She was provoking him to get him into the city. But how could Lilith have had Amanda watch that!

Lilith was now far behind him, squeezing between cars. Raphael's red sports car was nowhere in sight. He had passed her and his boss.

He had to get her on the open road. If he could knock her off the bike, she'd be vulnerable. Then he could run over the bitch. But he was way ahead of her. He had to goad *her*.

He got out of his car.

"You fucking dick!" cried a truck driver, lifting his arm out the window. "What the hell are you doing?" A few others shouted at him. That all ended when he brandished his pistol. Of course, Rick's observation was right. But he wasn't only running out of bullets, he was out. But Lilith wouldn't know that.

Cars were at a standstill as he ran to the middle lane. He pointed his pistol at the incoming motorcyclist. He was surprised she didn't pull out her gun. Maybe she had lost it, or it was out of bullets too? Then the bitch flipped him off again. She swerved between cars toward the outer right lane. She couldn't take the left shoulder as it ran right into a concrete barrier.

When she passed him, he sprinted back to his car. He jumped in and pursued her. She had likely bought his bluff, thinking he could still shoot her, and decided to get off the highway at the off-ramp.

Then they were back to the chase, only now they were driving down Van Nuys Boulevard running stoplights and avoiding near collisions.

And that's when he heard sirens. But they were driving too fast for the police to keep up.

He wasn't worried about cars. He was looking up at the sky. Straight overhead now, probably following him since his car accident on the highway, was a police helicopter. But that wasn't what he was afraid of either.

The light at the intersection ahead turned red. Lilith ran through the red light, coming an inch from hitting a car. She struggled to regain control of her bike, then a car in the other lane collided into her full speed. At this speed, the impact was tremendous and sent her bike spinning. She was ejected across the road.

John hit the brakes hard, trying to avoid oncoming traffic, right beside Lilith's bike.

Lilith was on the ground crawling. She was trying to get back on her motorcycle and ride off. John could run over her. All he had to do was hit the gas and run over her body.

He didn't. He threw his car door open. Then he ran to her before she could touch her cycle. He grabbed her. He pulled off her helmet and raised a fist to strike her. Her eyes were shut. She fell unconscious in his arms. Blood dripped from cuts along her face; worse, it was flowing from her chest.

There was the sound of metal smashing and horns honking around him. More accidents. John had stopped his car right in the middle of the road, and he was a sitting duck. Indeed, a car rode past nearly running them over. Then came sirens again, flashing red and blue, surrounding him.

John looked down at Lilith. She cracked open an eye.

"Fun," Lilith muttered with a laugh. She spit out blood. "That was fun, Azrael… Red or black? I've made my choice…have you? You and your twin bitch still green?" She chuckled a little as blood dripped from her lips. Then she closed her eyes and fell limp in his arms.

"Put your hands up!" cried an officer by megaphone.

John heard guns cock. He looked around him. He was surrounded.

"I said, put your hands up!" cried another officer. "Do it now!"

**26**

---

# INTERROGATION

AMANDA WASN'T ONE TO FEEL CLAUSTROPHOBIC. BUT sitting in a room with lime green walls, the size of a walk-in closet, across from one cop after the other was grating on her nerves. Especially since they had confiscated her phone and she had no idea what time it was. It smelled like cardboard. She could run her finger over a line of dust on the table. And it was quiet—too quiet. The walls were obviously soundproof. The only other piece of furniture in the empty room was a large single mirror against the wall. She suspected it was double sided, like in the movies.

Did John know that she didn't blame him? She had cried for what, she figured, hours? She hated John's enemies. But she didn't hate him. Yet somehow knowing him, his sternness, his intensity, knowing the man he was, she just knew he'd blame himself for her friend's death—if he had survived. Because he really was her guardian angel.

The doorknob moved. But no one opened the door.

She turned, looking at the green wall, and saw an image of Luane's body falling on an overpass bridge. The visions kept replaying over and over in her head.

An older man, dark-skinned and bald with a mustache,

finally entered. He sat down across from her, put a laptop on the table, and folded his hands before her.

"Amanda, my name's Officer Raymond. I'm the chief of police. We've questioned you all night. Now it's morning. Want some coffee?"

"No."

"We're hardly done."

"I told you everything I know," she said with a sigh, brushing back her hair. "Everything. My best friend's dead, okay? My friend's gone. And I don't know the woman who shot Luane. That answers every question you've asked, no matter how many times you guys ask me."

"You know what your friend did? Aside from complete mayhem for hundreds of Angelenos in their morning commute? His car was clocked by an officer around Wheeler Ridge driving over five hundred miles an hour. Do you know how fast a commuter jet flies? Around four hundred and fifty."

She shrugged.

"All my officers questioned you. I really have only one question. Who the hell is your friend?"

She turned from him. Again? *Seriously!*

"Amanda, who is he? I've never even heard of a car that drives like that. But I have over a hundred witnesses yesterday saying it did."

"I told you, but you don't believe me."

He ran his hand over his eyes. What, *he's tired? Really!* He opened his laptop. He waited for it to turn on, he typed something, then he looked up from the screen. "Angels. Like… Los Angeles?" he laughed. "Is this a joke?"

"I told you, but you don't believe me."

He leaned back in his chair, squinted at her, and typed something else. Coming from the computer, she recognized her voice.

*"Yeah, my guardian angel is back with me. He's back. Freaky as hell, I tell you, but kinda funny. He's the kind of guy who doesn't realize he's funny. He's wearing sunglasses in our hotel room. Inside the room. I'm not kidding. I mean, who the hell even does that? He says he's an angel—a dark angel. Doomed to walk this earth damning people by saving their lives. Would you like to say anything to my listeners, fallen angel?"*

*"Delete that."*


"Why did he want you to stop and delete that?"

"So you're not keeping me here because you suspect I was involved in the murder of my best friend?" she said, glaring at him. "You're keeping me here to find out secrets about the guy I was with?"

Amanda was fed up. Exhausted. She had never even talked back to an officer before, but these guys were relentless. And it was about the death of her best friend!

"A fallen angel?" the officer asked. Then he leaned back. "I almost believe it. That chase was something I've never seen before."

Just then the door opened again. A man in a black leather jacket and pants wearing shades walked in. At first, she thought it was John. But this man's skin was white as a ghost.

"What's the meaning of this?" the officer asked, jumping up.

"She's mine now," the man said. "This isn't your jurisdiction. She's mine to question."

"More questioning?" Amanda asked with a long sigh. *Fuck!*

It was a very pale version of the man Amanda had fallen in love with. But his skin was so white. He handed the chief of police a few papers. The officer read them, stood up, and nodded to Amanda.

"Nice meeting you," the police officer said. "I wish you could share more of your story."

Then he walked out.

And Amanda was alone with the creepy ghost version of her boyfriend. He sat down across the table like every other interrogator before him. But then he said offhand, "Of course, you're free."

"The others said it'd be only after paying bail."

"I paid it," the stranger said, flashing a grin. The grin was weird on a man wearing John's clothes. John never smiled like that. Then he reached out a hand to shake hers. She didn't touch it. "My name's Rick. Raphael in the language of your friend. I've been directing his work. How much did you tell them, Amanda?"

"Everything. That is, everything I know—which isn't much."

He laughed and leaned back in the plastic chair. "Honest to a fault, angel. Luckily, no one ever believes it."

"You guys are the angels."

"John would never have met you if you weren't an angel. But you weren't just pure. You were special to him. And John's enemies used that against him."

"Is he all right?"

"Yes. But he's in custody like you."

"He chased Lilith?"

"Lilith is dead."

"How?" Amanda asked, furrowing her brow. "I figured she was immortal or something."

"Only when she was on the bike. The archangels are immortal in their essence, but they take on a different soul in every life. One dies and another is reborn. The Lilith that you knew is dead."

"Well, that doesn't make a whole lot of sense. And you don't have to worry about me saying much to the cops because I can't understand most of what you guys tell me."

She leaned her head in her hands for a moment. She was so tired.

"You know John means a lot to me," Rick said. "You could almost say we're like brothers. There are few archangels and we work hard at what we do."

She looked up at him. He removed his shades. He had the same pink eyes as Lilith, and that creeped her out. He quickly put his shades back on. "I forget sometimes. Pardon me."

"You're albino?"

"No. All archangels have pale skin. The good and bad. But the similarity helps us a great deal as cover. Except Azraels. Azraels are closest to humans in appearance. White is divine. It represents the shining light of God. But evil is the twist and mockery of such purity. So even our enemies are pale."

"John's darkness seems closer to God than any of you."

"Hmm." He paused and stared at her from behind his shades. "Did John explain to you why he took a special interest in you?"

"No."

"He was instructed to save you in Arizona. That was all. Michael spared John from death from his past life and chose him to be the next Azrael. But he had a life before he was an archangel. They all do. He lived here in Los Angeles. The transformation from human to messenger took three decades for him. Even though he did not die, he might as well have been dead. When he returned everyone he had known was either old or had passed. His aunt, who had raised him, was long gone. So was his brother. Everyone in his family had left him.

"I was his one connection with his past world. You know what we do is secret. John could not confide in anyone other than me.

"Well, I warned him to never visit people from his past.

We get flashbacks and images, but we don't hold enough memories of our former lives to make a whole lot of sense of it. But if you're smart, like my Azrael, you can put pieces of the puzzle together."

"What are you getting at?" asked Amanda. She yawned. "I'm so tired." She shook her head. "I just want to go home."

"Do you know why John took a special interest in you, Amanda?" he asked again. "He had only just met you, but he guarded you with his life. Why? Why would he do that?" Rick chuckled. "Too innocent, he told me. He claimed you were too innocent." He shook his head. "I met up with John in a bar in Yuma a couple years ago. He was doing precisely what I suggested he never do—he was seeking someone from his past. I walked into the bar and met one of his dearest friends from his past. Her name was Sherry."

*Sherry. That name again.*

He nodded, as if understanding her recognition.

"Unbeknownst to me, Samael had followed us. So had Lilith. John saw them in time to run out and fight them outside the bar. Our archenemy did not see John's connection with Sherry… Or at least, that's what we thought at the time.

"Well, years later, John stopped Lilith from crashing her bike into your car and killing you in a car crash. That's when he met *you*. Sherry number two. The trap was set.

"They say everyone has a doppelgänger in the world. An identical twin. The job of our enemies is to stop us from saving the lives of pure souls. The best way to do that is to stop Azrael, or any of my other operatives, from doing their job. What better way than showing him an exact mirror image of his former lover and then threatening her life?" He gestured to her with a finger. "You, Amanda."

"Are you saying I look like John's former girlfriend?"

"No," Rick said, shaking his head. "No, that's not what

I'm saying. You don't look like her. You are a mirror image of her. You look exactly like her. He probably would have married Sherry had he not been taken from his former life. Do you understand what I'm saying, Amanda?"

*He doesn't love me. He loves Sherry.*

And now she felt more tired than ever. Maybe more tired than she had ever felt in her life. Deflated. Her best friend had died. And now her new lover only liked her because of a person she reminded him of.

"I'm sorry," Rick said.

"I don't know what else could go wrong," Amanda said, looking away. "Why are you telling me this?"

"John's alive. He'll get out of jail with my help. Then he'll seek you out. It's inevitable. You needed to know the truth." He smirked and looked right into her eyes. "For his sake, you need to stay away from him."

She looked at Rick suspiciously. "Wait a second. You want him back to work with you. And you want me out of the way."

"Amanda," he said, "going back to—"

"I don't care if I look like her," Amanda snapped. "I felt something with him. And I know he does with me. And I also don't care if it messes up your little arrangement of fucking over angels from going to heaven."

She stood up.

"Michael will have his Azrael," Rick snapped, jumping up too. "You can't stop John from doing what he was put on this Earth to do."

"I thought you were here to help me," she said, shaking her head. "I can't figure out which of you is good or evil. You seem like a sadistic devil right now. You said he was your friend? What would he think about you telling me to stay away from him?"

"I do care about him."

"But not his happiness, I think." She looked at the door. "Can I leave? You said I was free to go."

He shook his head. "I have to tell you one more thing."

"To hurt me?" she snapped.

"No. Good news. Your friend, Luane, survived the gunshot. She's in critical condition in the ICU, but she's alive. And the doctors there think she'll probably survive."

Then Amanda felt the most foreign thing she had felt in twenty-four hours of questioning: a smile.

"Believe me or not, I didn't come here to hurt you, Amanda. I came to free you. But, yes, you're smart like John. I want my operative back."

"That's not up to me or you. That's up to John."

He gestured for her to exit through the door. Then he shook his head. "Actually, it's up to you. If you show up in his life again, as the young version of his lover, you only torture him. And endanger both of you. I tell you, you have to stay away from him."

## 27

# MICHAEL

John sat in an uncomfortable green plastic chair against the wall of a small interrogation room. The walls were beige. The wood table before him had a sheet of white dust. He had been alone for hours, perhaps a day. When the cell door opened, he expected to see another cop. It wasn't. It was Michael.

Michael was the calmest being John had ever encountered. His face seemed incapable of trouble. His pale face and pink eyes were the warmest and kindest he had ever known. Whereas Samael and Lilith were monsters, Michael's countenance was the definition of peace. And as he approached, he even seemed to glide more than walk.

When John had first met Michael, he had seemed like a vision. He had long white feathery wings and wore a white cloth that seemed to blend with his skin. Not today. Today, Michael wore a black suit.

He sat down in the chair across from John.

"I always liked you," Michael said. "In an eternity of souls, yours brooded, but shone forth the most. And I always wondered why you hid your shining light? Perhaps the light that lies in your heart is too strong and must be darkened?"

"I've done everything you asked," John replied. "You said that if I saved enough angels, I could pass peacefully. I think the hundreds I saved would have been enough by now. Now this is where I am destined to be? I ask for what you promised."

"Those that serve God never ask how much good they need to do, John," Michael said, raising a finger. "They just do it. You've also been asked to kneel. You have yet to do that."

John leaned forward. "Fuck you."

"I'm here to explain," Michael continued, unperturbed. "Giving you a position as Azrael enabled you to purify your heart. Samael gambled with God over your soul. He found you the likeness of your lover. He did this for two reasons. To lure you away from being a guardian messenger. The other was far more insidious. Personal. You were told that if you saved enough souls you'd be brought to the gates of heaven. Yes, I told you that. Well, what if I told you that if you hadn't sacrificed for Amanda, *that* would have destined you to wander? Forever, driving you to perdition? Your heart chose Amanda. That was the correct choice."

"Why play games with me?"

"Why ask *me*?" Michael smiled. Then he shook his head. "I don't make the rules. What makes you think that you're the only Azrael? Perhaps everyone on the edge of death must be tested?"

"So these past years were just another test? If it's an illusion, what makes you any less evil than Lilith or Samael?"

"Evil is merely the shadow of light. There is only love. But there is blindness. That is all that lies within Adamah."

"Fuck off," John said, standing up and rubbing his eyes.

"Don't play with my head with words. Why are you even here?"

"To give truth." And he smiled back. "Now sit down. I'm about to tell you good news."

"Give it to me and then leave me alone."

John didn't sit. He thought of Amanda. He thought of how he had failed in saving her best friend. He should never have given her even the pretense of victory. The rescue was doomed from the start. Although he had told her that, he felt like he had failed to convince her.

"Your name is not John," Michael said. "You know nothing of your past. Everything you know comes from Sherry."

"I've seen images."

"Fleeting. You were a good field officer before you died. I stress *good*." Michael leaned forward, looking up. "John, you were never a fallen angel. You weren't a demon. Azrael stands at the border between life and death. If you were destined for hell, God wouldn't have tested you at all." He leaned back in his chair. "Everyone who dies goes through judgment. Theirs is based on their past. You were an agent. So we watched you do your job. But others who die are tested differently. Now, because you chose Amanda and her friend, you are free. You can ascend." Michael grinned. It was a genuine smile, but it didn't make John feel any better. "You acted selflessly. You risked your soul for hers. For the height of such sacrifice, you may ascend." He raised a finger to the ceiling. "If that is your wish."

"Why wouldn't it be? And how do you know I didn't choose her because of her looks? Her similarity to Sherry?"

"That's Samael talking. You didn't help Amanda because of her looks, did you?" Michael shook his head and smiled. "Look behind you, brother, if looks are what you desire."

John turned. He was blinded by light. He missed not

having his shades to block it from his eyes. But then he felt a release. All his fears and pain seemed to leave his body as he squinted before the brilliant light. It was the most pleasurable brilliance he had ever known, as bright as the sun. Perhaps brighter. The strange thing is he had seen this light before. He hadn't recalled this until now. When Michael had met him upon death, he had seen Michael in this light.

"All you need to do is walk through now."

John got up and walked to the wall, now an open portal. But his arm was grabbed from behind. John turned back and felt sick just looking behind him. He saw the dark shade of Michael still in the jail cell. Michael always shone light, but now the archangel seemed dark.

"Know this, brother," said Michael. "If you leave, you won't be able to help those you leave behind. Samael now plans to take the life of your lover. It is in retribution for the death of his love, Lilith. Every action in your past world has consequences. You have this last choice. You may either ascend or drop back down and help her." Michael touched his shoulder. "Angel down, John. This time it's her. But you are free. I suggest you head to the light. Your job as Azrael is over."

John hesitated. Then he blurted out, almost in a shout, "another test!"

"Think carefully," Michael said with a nod. "The consequence of going back and trying to save her is returning to purgatory. Even saving and good constitute desire. In purgatory, the fight remains. It is a world of darkness and pain. And God shall judge you. I suggest you walk through the light."

"Open the door."

"Which one? Gabriel gives you this gnosis. I told him it's cruel. Only the light is the right decision, John. Retire and end this. End this now."

"Before I leave, Michael," John asked, "tell me why the

pure are taken before all others? Amanda reminded me, and I never understood. Why would devils take the innocent?"

"You and Raphael save the virtuous angels on Earth from death. But if peace will reign upon death, why does God not simply permit suicide? Or will it? Why keep anyone alive at all? Why not retire all souls to heaven? And why do I call you good for keeping the pure from ascending to God?"

"I was asking you."

"And yet you make your choice. It seems you already know."

**28**

---

# THE HOSPITAL

Luane blinked her eyes and squinted under the light as Amanda squeezed her hand. This wasn't the first time she had opened her eyes, but it was the first time she'd had that awful tube out of her mouth. It seemed like Amanda had tried to talk to her for hours. Now Amanda had just returned from the hospital cafeteria.

Then Luane did what Amanda had waited for all night. She smiled.

"I won't ask you how you're feeling," Amanda said.

Luane groaned.

"Like shit, huh?"

Amanda put down another garland of daisies she had bought for her friend at the gift shop. Daisies were Luane's favorite. Then she sat by the bedside, brushed Luane's hair from her eyes, and took her hand. "I'm so happy you're all right, you don't even know."

"I don't feel all right, Mands."

Amanda tried to smile. Then she fought with herself not to cry. She wanted to be strong for her friend.

"At least you can speak," Amanda said, patting her hand.

Luane nodded. But then she didn't say anything. She turned and closed her eyes again. After a little while, she muttered quietly, "Who was she, Mands? She kept naming you with such hatred."

"Who?"

"You know," Luane said, rolling her eyes. Yeah, she was back to being the Lu Amanda loved.

"Someone I met on my trip," Amanda said. "If I told you who she is, you wouldn't believe me. But my friend got revenge. So you can be happy about that. With all your pain, she felt more, I'm sure."

"I never would have thought *I'd* be in trouble from your stupid road trip." Then she winced. "Fuck, my head feels like it's ready to explode."

"Do you know the chances of that bullet not blowing up all the important stuff between your ears? The doctor told me you're a miracle." Amanda chuckled. "Hmm, a miracle. Yeah, maybe my friend had something to do with that too. I'm just so happy you're alive."

"I don't think I really want to meet your friends."

Amanda nodded. Then she got up and gestured to a small table by the bed and showed her the flowers. "Got you daisies."

Luane turned slowly. "Thanks, babe."

"I still owe you your cactus. It was destroyed twice."

"When I'm better, I want to hear all about your adventures, okay? Just…not now. Fuck, it hurts, so bad."

"You want me to tell the nurse?"

"I'm maxed out on morphine," she said, shaking her head. Then she feebly lifted a handheld wire with a button.

"Well, you can just listen to my podcast later. It's live."

"Okay, Amanda," she said with a laugh. "But stop. Stop being you."

"You want me to let you sleep?"

Luane shook her head. Then she touched her hand. "I want you to be here."

And that did it. That made the tears finally come. She couldn't control it.

"What's wrong?" Luane asked.

"Nothing. Everything. God, I thought I lost you."

"It's okay. The doctors think I'll be better soon. It's just gonna take time. Come here." And Lu reached out her arms. Amanda hugged her gently.

And they both cried together.

"Crying's okay if it's joyful, right?" Amanda whispered in Luane's ear. "I'm crying because you're alive."

"Everything's going to be okay."

"Yes. But it's all my fault."

"Well," she said, pushing her back. Luane smiled. "I really can't wait to hear how it's your fault."

"It's on my podcast."

"Shut up." But then she laughed again. She laughed a little too hard and it made her clutch her head in pain. "We're gonna be okay," she said, squeezing Amanda's hand again. "You and I. Everything is going to be okay now."

*Hmm... Not if I tell her where I'm going next weekend.*

## 29

# THE HUNTER

That officer named Rick had told Amanda that John was in Yuma. She remembered him saying Yuma. So Amanda figured all she had to do was drive near Yuma. It wasn't that far from LA. And it wasn't a big town. Of course, she had asked John for his number. He had typed it in her phone. The contact was fake, of course.

*Maybe he never wanted to keep contact with you. But then why did he keep saving me? Why risk his job, his life, his soul, to help me? Of course he cares about me. He does. He fucking loves me. And, well, I love him.*

She'd head exactly in the same direction she had when she began her dangerous adventure, only she had to rent a car. And she had to make sure not to tell Luane. Or her parents. Or anyone. But, whereas witnessing the desert had been breathtaking before, *resplendent*, now it reminded her of all the horrors of her recent trip. And although Luane was blessedly, fantastically, wonderfully feeling better, Amanda couldn't keep getting visions of her being shot on that bridge. She had never hated overpasses as much as she did now.

She shook her head and took out her recorder to get her mind off that.

"Guys, I want to say a huuugge THANK YOU to all of you for supporting me this past week over the recovery of my friend. You heard my unbelievable story. So many of you came to me with support regarding the assault. Well, with that, it's with beyond *ecstaticness"—Is ecstaticness a word? Oh well, it should be—"*It's with ecstaticness that I tell you that Luane is feeling better. Yeah! Ain't that amazing! She's gonna make it out of this alive. And, aside from a headache, without much of a scratch. Still beautiful. Still Lu. I really couldn't be happier. God's shining over us with this miracle. I feel blessed. And I'm… I'm so happy.

"So…whatcha doing now, Amanda?"

"Driving.

"Where?

"You know I fell in love with that guy in Colorado, right?" She laughed. "Well, I'm gonna go find him. So, although it's with fucking-nail-biting-white-fisted-terror that I'm driving back to where it all started, I'm back on the highway in Arizona. Do you remember? Arizona. Yeah, I'm heading back to where there's red sand and cacti the size of people everywhere. I know, crazy right? I heard he lives in a small city out here. Yuma." She bent forward for a better view of the desert in every direction along the horizon. "Somewhere. Well, if he does, I'll find him. I'm just glad he doesn't live in Manhattan."

Click. *That's enough.* Then she sighed.

*Shit, but what if I can't find him?*

So she clicked her recorder back on.

"Okay, I lied…sort of. I always told you guys I'd be honest. Well, Caligirl gettingold24 also has an interview to go to in Phoenix. Can you believe that! It was delayed because of the horror that befell my friend, but they still want to interview me for a newspaper. How fucking exciting is that?! So, win or lose, I'll come home with something. A job? Maybe. How about a hot tall dark stranger? You never know. Maybe both. We'll see if I can get everything I desire—Lu back to her crazy self, a new job, and that hunk of a man. What do you guys think?"

Click. She laughed again. Then she nodded, satisfied at her work. That was a far better ending.

The beauty of the Arizona desert unfolded again, as she rode over a red summit, with those same saguaros on red soil by the shoulder of the highway and the bright yellow sun rising on the horizon. Then a large bird soared above, just like before. Seeing the bird somehow made her think he'd be here. She leaned forward for a better look at the majestic bird. Then she looked back at an infinite dark horizon behind her. All she saw was the desert and an incoming semi-truck riding far behind. She had slowed down on her lookout, driving near the speed limit. The truck passed and left open road behind her. Then…nothing. Just open desert with the rising sun.

She tapped on her steering wheel to the music of the band GTR.

*Stupid. This is stupid. So you see a bird and you think your stranger will be here?*

*Well, maybe birds herald angels?*

*Don't be stupid. There's a lot of birds out in the desert.*

*Not mine. That one looks like mine.*

She jumped as her cell phone vibrated in her pocket. She reached forward and hit speaker mode on her Bluetooth console.

"Hey, babe," said Luane. She sounded so weak.

"How are you feeling?"

"Like shit. The pain comes in waves. I was shot in the head, you know. I was hoping you could bring over my air pods. I want to listen to some music and kinda escape."

"Oh, good. You must be feeling better then, Lu. But

listen, I can't come today. I'll try to be back tomorrow night to get it for you."

"Where'd you run off to?"

"My interview."

"Oh yeah. Oh yeah. You heading to LAX now? Good luck, babe. Forget the music. I'll get Ben to bring them over. I so hope you get that job. You deserve it. And have a great flight. I'm… I'm gonna go back to sleep."

"Okay, Lu. Love you."

"Bye, babe."

There's no way she'd tell her where she was now. It wasn't the airport, that was for sure. She leaned forward and searched for her bird again.

*Okay, Guardian Angel, where in heaven are you?*

The soaring bird hovered over her again. With yellow rays now lighting the surrounding vista, the bird sort of glowed.

But then the bird darted away. It seemed something had scared it off.

In her rearview mirror, she spotted the reason. A shiny black motorcycle was rapidly approaching. Too rapid. It was riding at incredible speed, vanishing down a dip in the road and then popping up again, seemingly riding a mile a minute. She hadn't seen the motorcycle behind her before. It had just appeared. Worse, it looked like the shiny black bikes that had followed her in Kansas and Cincinnati. The biker's clothes and helmet were the same pitch black. The only good thing she noticed as it approached was that the biker didn't have long white hair.

When close to the rear of her white rental car, the biker started doing that leaning back and forth aggressive stupid thing that Lilith used to do. Then the bike accelerated right beside her window. With a gloved hand, he hit the driver's window hard and pointed for her to pull over.

*Not this time.*

Amanda drove right into him. The bike swerved a little then recovered on the road. Amanda turned sharply into the bike again. But the stranger's bike just kept bouncing off her car.

The biker rode in front of her and slammed on his brakes. Amanda hit the gas. She had sworn to herself that if she landed in danger again, she wouldn't be intimidated. She'd go headlong into it. So that's what she did now. She *literally* drove into it. Finally, by the impact, the biker was thrown like a billiard ball to the opposite side of the highway. But somehow it shook and regained control again. Then he shot in front of her, pumping the brakes again. And so, yet again, Amanda braced for impact. She had searched for her angel in the desert but had found a devil instead.

Amanda looked at her speedometer. Although she kept colliding into the bike, her speed was dropping. He was succeeding in slowing her down. What would he do when he stopped her car?

*Kill me.*

There was no barrier by this part of the highway. So Amanda turned her car sharply and floored it. She slid over gravel and sand with the bike still in front of her. She saw the biker turn around to chase her. Then she drifted all over the place, performing an extremely dangerous three-sixty in the middle of the highway. Her maneuver was so sharp that she worried her rental would roll over. After swerving back and forth on the opposite side of the highway, she finally recovered. Then she caught a red flash in her rearview mirror. She initially thought it was just glare from the rising sun. It wasn't. It was a bright red flash and, when it was close enough, it materialized into a car behind her: a sleek red sports car, like a Ferrari. Not John's black one. Was it John? Was he driving a red car now?

The sports car rammed the biker behind her, but unlike

Amanda's collisions, it hit the biker at great speed. The biker recovered and tried to ram into Amanda's passenger side, but then the red car hit it again. This time, the red car didn't relent, pushing the bike all the way onto the shoulder. The biker slid off the freeway as the car ran over him.

Looking in her rearview mirror, Amanda saw the driver, wearing black clothes and shades like John's, jump out of the car. It wasn't John. His skin was pale and his hair was short and white. He pulled out a pistol and shot the biker dead.

Amanda accelerated, pushing her rental car as fast as it could go. That's when she noticed a large piece of metal jutting from her hood. The car drove a bit wobbly too. But at this point she didn't fucking care.

The red car soon trailed her again. Then it flashed red and blue lights, as if it were a police car. But the police don't execute bikers. So she didn't stop.

Quickly, seemingly impatiently, the red car zoomed up to her driver's side. The dark passenger side window rolled down. The guy cried out, "Pull your car over. Now!"

Amanda recognized him. It was Rick, that officer she had met in the interrogation room.

She pulled over.

He jumped out of his car and ran to her. "What are you doing here!" he cried. He was so loud, she heard him through her closed windows.

She rolled down the window.

"I'm driving on my way to an interview."

Rick took his shades off. Then he glared at her with his pink eyes, as if she were absolutely crazy. Well, maybe she was. "Your interview is in Phoenix, Amanda."

"How do you know that?"

He leaned into her window. With the red and blue lights behind her, for a second, she felt like reaching in her purse and handing him her driver's license.

"How the hell do you know about my interview?" Amanda asked again.

"Amanda, what are you doing here on Interstate Eight? Phoenix is off of Interstate Ten."

"A detour."

He didn't let up, staring at her with his pink eyes.

"Okay, fine," Amanda said, rolling her eyes and laughing. "You got me. I'm looking for him. I thought maybe he'd be around here. But it's still on the way."

"Why don't you step out of the car. Come take a look."

"Is it safe?"

He nodded. Then he looked back at the highway in the direction of their chase.

She didn't want to get out, but she reached over to open the driver's side door. She couldn't open it. The car door was jammed. Rick sighed and heaved her door open.

The first thing she did was stand up straight and look at herself. She checked her shorts and T-shirt. No blood this time from her nose. She wasn't damaged.

Her car was. There were large gray metal gashes all over the side and front of the car. The white paint had been sheared off. One of the rear doors was completely dented in. Her door might have been jammed, but the passenger door was caved in. The front hood was bent. That's why there was a piece of metal jutting out.

She laughed and shrugged. "Good thing I gave them my credit card. The car's covered with my insurance."

"Amanda, go home," Rick said. He put his shades back on.

"Not sure I can now," she said with another chuckle. "Don't know if it's drivable. But I think I'm getting used to danger around you guys."

He gazed up at the rising sun. He reminded her so much of John. He wore the same black jacket with jeans. He was a good-looking man. And his red car was amazing. Of course, there was no sign of any damage to his car.

"We only delayed them," he said.

"Where's John?"

"I don't know," he said, shaking his head. "I've been looking for him too. Maybe he's ascended? We put out code bulletins when angels fall. We sent one to him. He's not answering. I haven't heard from him since he was arrested."

"Can you give me his number? I can try to get a hold of him."

"Amanda, stop." He finally turned to her. "This is serious. If he wanted you to contact him, he would have given it to you."

She felt her curled lip turn to a frown.

"You're so much like her," Rick said, shaking his head. Then he looked out at the horizon.

"What'd ya mean, he might have ascended?"

"I've heard his care for you was looked on positively by Michael and Gabriel. It seems his compassion for you might have been enough to finally free his soul. I don't know." Rick looked back toward the rising sun. "I hope so for his sake." Then he looked back at her car and shook his head. "You need help after this wreck. Just—"

"I'll call triple A."

"Then you'll be dead by nightfall. You think that was the only angel out here? He was a scout. Come into my car. I'll drive you back to LA."

"I think I'll take my chances and call triple A."

He grabbed her arm.

"Don't fucking touch me!" Amanda snapped, looking at his hand. "Don't you ever do that!"

"Amanda, you need protection. I'll take you back to LA."

"And I told you, I have an interview."

"Forget the interview." Then he squinted at her. She could just make it out behind the sunglasses. He seemed to scrutinize her. "I tell you what. I'm heading where John would be, if he's here. It's close enough. If you came here to find John, I'll take you to the one place where he *might* be. You can be safe there before you head back home. Is that enough for you to come with me?"

"Maybe. Where?"

"Sherry's. I need to scope out her place too and make sure she's okay. It'll be a quick stop. It's right near here. But then I'm driving you back. It's up to you. I think you need to speak to her, anyway. She might knock some sense into you."

"You got a deal, mister. I'll hitch a ride in that little thing of yours. Interview's not till tomorrow anyway." She smirked. Then she walked over to her trunk. The trunk was fine. It was the only part of the car not dented. Then she took out her large suitcase. "You sure you'll have room in that little car?"

"Do you have sunglasses in your bag?" he asked.

That was enough to erase her smugness. She found herself shaking.

Rick chuckled. "Yeah. Don't worry."

**30**

---

# INFIDEL

JOHN STOOD OVER A CLIFFSIDE WATCHING THE RISING yellow and red rays brighten the valley, which was sandy and filled with weeds. He had his sunglasses off and he waited as the yellow rays slowly rose over this blessed place, this sanctuary. He let the rays blind him. The sun reminded him of the light Michael had shown him in that interrogation room, but it was dimmer and without peace, only providing warmth to his body. He didn't avert his gaze, wouldn't avert it, despite the risk of harm. Like in the myth of Phaeton, he stared at it and let warmth wash over him. But unlike the light Michael had shown him, this one only gave him pain and worry.

He looked down at the ravine. It was nearly a three-hundred-foot drop.

He tried his phone again. He called the code name "Hunter." Again, there was no answer.

Then he turned at the sound of a bird. It had landed on his hood and was fluttering its wings over his black car.

～

"She's in the living room," said a voice to his left.

John turned around. There was a bright vision of Sherry, transparent but glowing before the view of the desert valley. She was smiling sadly. A younger version of Sherry. Amanda.

"She needs you now." She hugged him. A tear ran down her cheek.

"There's nothing I can do."

"Just be here. That's all she needs."

Rooms appeared beyond a grand foyer. They were familiar. It was dark inside. He remembered now that his aunt had always kept the lights off in her mansion. Now she sat on a couch and just stared out into the void, not saying a thing. She didn't even seem to recognize him as he walked inside. But then, as he sat on the old fluffy couch beside her, she leaned her head on his shoulder and wept.

"I missed you," his aunt said.

"I'm sorry it took me so long to be back."

"We know," she said. She forced a swallow and turned to him, patting his hand. Then she reached for his shades, but he didn't let her take them. "Stay with me. He was your brother."

"He was my cousin."

"He was your brother. But all is well now that I see you here and safe. And he will be in a better place in heaven. Will you say words at the ceremony?"

"If that is what you want."

"Of course it is." She turned to him and examined his face. "Take your glasses off." He obliged. Then she examined his eyes. "What's the matter? What are you feeling, son?"

"Anger. Anger for him getting involved with the jerks he did. I told you and I warned him to stay away. Anger for the pain it's causing you."

"But what good is anger?" She reached for his hand,

but he pulled away this time. She forced a smile. Then she brushed her hand over his short hair. "Let it go. This isn't one of the enemies you can beat. I have you. And I have Sherry. All will be well now."

"Nothing will be well anymore."

"Through prayer, I have learned that there is no end. Only light in darkness. Let that gem of a woman you found be your light. She is such a treasure. Let her light your way, like God."

"I don't believe in God."

"It would make you less angry." She took his hand gently and he sat beside her again. Then she said softly, leaning on his arm, "He was your brother. And I love him. Just as I love you, my son."

Then she cried again.

He heard crying from someone else too. Not just from his aunt on his shoulder. It was from the younger Sherry, who was still standing in the other room by the front door, close enough for him to hear her weeping.

John put his shades back on.

"I have you. And I have Sherry," she said again. "All will be well now."

There was a shriek from a large bird. The bird fluttered its wings and took off from the hood of his black car. He remembered that memory of his mother now. He watched the bird soar the hundreds of feet down into the desert and disappear into the light of the sun. And John put on his shades once more, just as he had in the vision.

Then he got back in his car. He listened to a voicemail message sent by his organization and forwarded to him during the night. It was Gabriel's voice.

"Angel down. Sherry. White. Sixty-two. Born a Pisces.

Working near Yuma at Angel Dive. Exercise extreme caution. Marked by Samael. If you're still around, we need you, Azrael."

Usually the APB was put out by Rick. What had happened to his boss?

He called Rick again.

No answer.

John looked back at the bright sun.

*Let it go. This isn't one of your enemies you can beat. I have you. And I have Sherry. All will be well now.*

"All is not well now, Mother."

He reversed his car. Then he hit the gas, drifted across the sand along the cliffside, and re-entered the highway.

**31**

———

# THE DEVIL'S SERMON

Amanda found Sherry's place to be secluded, miles from downtown. Amid desert shrubs and sand stood a one-story building. The walls were windowed, kind of reminding Amanda of the diner in Kansas. To her left, if she looked hard enough with binoculars, she could probably find downtown Yuma on the two-lane road. The structure was simple and clean, its wood exterior painted red. There were hubcaps hung on wood columns by the entrance and old metal garage signs advertising gas and oil products. The automobile motif was a perfect fit for John. But Rick's red luxury car hardly fit the place's simplicity.

It looked deserted. Even though it was midday, their cars and an old blue pickup were the only vehicles parked on a dusty, broken-up asphalt parking lot.

Rick opened the front door. Then Amanda was instantly engulfed in smoke from inside. It wasn't cigarettes. It smelled like the place had been lit on fire. The light was dim and country music was playing, but they were the only ones there. The walls were painted burgundy, almost auburn, and decorated with lots of silly stuff like antlers, dart boards, and sports jerseys. And at the far end, through the smoke, was a large wooden bar. It was there that the wall was blackened. The charred wall was emanating all the smoke. There was an empty stage in another corner, empty except for an acoustic guitar leaning on a stool. Wooden tables with matching wooden chairs were vacant. But a few chairs were lying on the ground with their legs in pieces. And broken glass was strewn along the floor near the bar.

Amanda gasped. A shadow moved through the smoke near the counter. Rick noticed it too and touched his gun holster, slung over his T-shirt under his jacket. He pulled out the pistol. Then Amanda jumped when she saw the stranger—a woman with long white hair in a tight black leather motorcycle suit. Lilith.

*How?!*

"Took you long enough, Hunter," Lilith said. "But I expected Azrael. Well, you and she will do."

"Where's Sherry?" Rick asked.

"Right beside you," Lilith said with a chuckle.

"I thought you died?" Amanda asked.

"I thought I captured you," Lilith said with a shrug. "This is all very confusing, Sherry." She walked around the counter and approached them. Rick pointed his gun at the devil.

"It's Samael," Rick said, cocking his head back to Amanda.

"I thought Samael was a man?" Amanda said.

"I can take any shape I please, darling," said Lilith. "And, until I restore the beloved lamia you helped slay, I shall pay my respects by using her form. And now that I have you, I can kill both you *and* your older self."

She walked up close to Rick. Amanda felt her skin crawl when the woman's pink eyes flashed red as she glared at him. "Put the gun down, Raphael, or she dies.

There's no need to break my body. I will simply take another."

"What's your game, Samael?" Rick asked. "What are you doing to my friend?"

"*We all have friends, don't we!*" she shouted in his face. But the shout wasn't what made Amanda jump. It was her voice. Her voice had turned deep, like a man's. "I lost Lilith! Now I have both the old and the young Sherry. If I'm lucky, they'll both pass away right before Azrael's fucking eyes!"

"You brought Amanda into John's life long before he killed Lilith," Rick said.

"I did, didn't I?" she said, her voice calming and returning to female. "I did." Then she walked up to Amanda. "So I did. Well, we had to test our Azrael, didn't we?"

"You shot my friend in the head!" snapped Amanda.

"Such courage," Lilith said with a nod. "The devil stands before you, but you hold yourself with pride. Bravery? Or is it stupidity? So like your older self."

"Where is she?" repeated Rick, raising the gun to Lilith's head.

"Right in front of you," Lilith quipped. "Does it matter? To humans, if the body is there and there is a glimmer of a resemblance, it's all the same. No one looks further than the face. Isn't that right, Amanda? What lies underneath is really of no consequence."

"The only thing stopping me from pulling the trigger, Samael," Rick said, "is your information. I need you to tell me where Sherry is. Where's the *older* one?"

"Transmutable, undeniable, manifested in God's glory right before your very eyes, Raphael, Sherry stands before you. Younger, but still the same vessel." Lilith raised a finger, and then she looked deep into Amanda's eyes with fiery bright red ones. "When you were younger, Sherry, you wanted to be a journalist. It was 1984. But you fell in love with an officer and during heroic duty on a secret mission, the man you loved died. Distraught, but with the funds left to you from the death of your well-to-do man, you decided to create this…" She gestured to the room. "This dump, instead of furthering your writing career. Azrael influenced you even then. You built this restaurant for sinful drifters, loners and alcoholics, because it reminded you of him. Angel Dive. And I reveled in it. I think it was because it was a place to remember the greatest drifter of all. Your guardian. My Azrael. That nothing. That zero. John."

Amanda was trembling in shock. Lilith's long hair shortened. Her jawbone hardened. Her brows moved out. Her skin dried. And she grew a beard. Lilith's beauty was transformed into a pale male version of herself.

"Not all is what it appears," the demon said now with a low male voice. "You may chase me through the firmament, Hunter, but I will never stop. Shoot me down, I return. So put your gun down. Because *I* can kill *you.*"

"Where's the angel down?" asked Rick again. "Where's Sherry?"

"Sherry is hardly an angel down," Samael said with a laugh. "The only angel here was Amanda, before he fucked her." Then he raised a finger. "Or was she?"

He walked right up to Amanda and gazed upon her face again. Then he purred before her as she lurched back.

"Tell me now, Samael," warned Rick.

"Tell you what? Look behind you, idiot," Samael said, cocking his head back. "Let me finish my sermon or you'll never speak another goddamn word again."

The empty parking lot behind the windows was now filled with black motorcycles. The weirdest thing was that Amanda hadn't heard them approach outside.

"What makes a vessel pure, Amanda?" Samael asked. "Hmm? That is the question for the eons. The answer, I tell you, will open the door to heaven to you. Would you like to know? Would you like me to tell you?" He touched her cheek with a black-gloved finger. She lurched back. "I don't enjoy speaking with him. You're softer."

Rick cocked his gun and pressed it close to Samael's head.

"Zero," Samael said with a chuckle to Amanda. "Nothing. Absolutely nothing can purify you. There is no struggle on Adamah. I've already won. None of you will approach the purity of your so-called God. There is no return to the garden, just as there are no angels. That is the answer that all of you animals run from.

"It makes not a difference in the world what a cock fucks. It makes not a difference in the world what neighbor is strangled. It makes not a difference under the firmament if you worship God, graven images, swear, say the lord's name in vain, never go to church, kill your mother, fuck her or your neighbor, break her dog's neck, steal the clothes on her back." His eyes widened and shone red at Amanda. "It matters not. It makes no difference at all! For there are no angels. No angels, just as there is no God. There is nothing. Zero!" He stopped his tirade for a moment to catch a breath. "Oh, you can pray. You can do that. Ask forgiveness for your sins from your so-called lord with the vain hope of protection. But behold my occult. When you are alone in the dark, you won't find God. Oh, no. You'll find me. Nothing. Just as there is a man with no name called John. There is nothing. Absolutely nothing, Sherry!" The beast smirked at her. She cringed as his eyes glowed red. "You shall suffer eternally for my gnosis. That is my commandment for you and your kin. Your only recourse is to worship my rising star. For I will rise, as surely as dawn falls."

"So pretty—" The devil's voice eerily returned to Lilith's. "So pretty." He reached for her face with his gloved fingers again, but she backed away. "You're very pretty, pretty, Sherry. I see what he once saw in you."

"Are you finished?" asked Rick.

"Oh, I haven't begun," Samael said with his low voice returning. "He comes. Let us play his cops and robbers game, shall we? I bring *hers*. The damage Azrael shall cause in the name of love you may only blame on yourselves. Gabriel heralded him onto Adamah once more, rather than Michael ascend him. So comes choice. Love. And for this vapid thing called love, the greatest desire of all, I shall greet him with pain." Samael looked outside over Rick's shoulder. He lifted a gloved hand over his head and then closed it. "He works for me now."

Amanda heard a few cracks and then a crash of glass from a window. It was gunfire. Before she knew it, Rick fell to the ground. Shot dead? She couldn't tell. It was so fast. But she hadn't even seen Samael brandish a weapon.

She fell to the floor and shook Rick's shoulders, but his eyes were closed and he was unresponsive. From the corner of her eye, she saw Samael rush past her through the front door.

"Take the girl," he ordered.

She was grabbed. Amanda kicked and shouted, trying to swing at the person holding her, but whoever held her, held her tight. No, it was several people. She made out a few of the bikers in black jumpsuits clutching her. They dragged her through the dusty parking lot to the blue pickup. There they tied her hands and gagged her. Then they threw her in the back of the truck.

Lying on her side, she saw another woman with hands tied behind her back. Then the stranger stared at her probably with as much disbelief as she felt. It was her twin, only so much older than she was.

Bikers closed the pickup door. And the car drove off,

drifting, hardly being easy on her body as she hit the metal sides on turns.

Lying on her side, Amanda couldn't see anything over the truck, only her older self. And her older self, with long gray hair, seemed to be trying to smile under her taped mouth. It was as if her twin was trying to say something. It was as if Sherry was trying to comfort her.

**32**

———

# MIRROR

THE RIDE WAS BUMPY AS HELL EVEN THOUGH AMANDA figured she was being driven on the highway. Her shoulder and back kept banging against the metal back of the pickup. And there was a lot of noise from the wind and motorcycles revving, but she couldn't see a thing above Sherry's head. The old woman was oddly squirming like crazy, lurching her back up and grunting for some reason. Maybe she was sick. The whole drive was nauseating.

Amanda turned her body and stared for a moment at the vibrating metal wheel hub, to look for something, anything, to calm her stomach. But that was more sickening. So she swung back and gazed at her granny look-alike. That's when she finally realized what her companion was doing. She was working the ropes over her wrists. And she was almost free! The rope was dangling on one arm. Then she was back to squirming until she freed a hand. Then she rolled onto her knees and yanked the tape off her mouth.

"Be quiet," Sherry said. "And stay down."

*What the hell do you think I'm going to do? I can barely move.*

Sherry was pulling at the ropes around Amanda's wrists.

"Next time you get tied up," Sherry said right in Amanda's ear, "press your hands together, keep your wrists apart, and tighten your muscles. That'll keep it loose. Shit, this is tight."

Amanda felt a hand get free.

"Stay still!" Sherry said in a forced whisper. "And keep down." Then she reached for her face. "This is gonna hurt. Sorry. No yells, 'kay?"

Amanda nodded. Then…rip, the tape was torn off her face.

*Oww!*

But she didn't say a word. Sherry smiled and nodded.

"Thank you." Amanda nodded. "How'd you know how to do that?"

"You think this is the first time that big oaf got me captured? Let me tell you something, hanging 'round John is always trouble." She smiled again, though a bit more morosely. Then she examined Amanda's face. And that was weird because it felt like she was staring in the mirror. "Now I get it. Damn, I forgot how good I used to look. You're very beautiful, Amanda. Or I was."

"Thanks a lot, I think. So, do we like just jump for it?"

"No." Sherry shook her head. "We have to time this just right. Those jerks will shoot you. Keep your head down and hold the rope close by your wrists so if they glance over, it'll look like you're still tied up." She looked up, squinting at the sun. "I'm not worried about us. I'm worried about him."

"They're trapping him again?"

She nodded.

"This isn't the first time they've used me to get to him," Amanda said. "Where are they taking us?"

Sherry put a finger over her lips. She gazed up at the shaking metal wall. She was listening for something. But all

Amanda heard was the sound of revving motorcycles and the rush of the road.

"I'm not sure," Sherry finally answered. Then she furrowed her brow. "Why are you here, anyway? John said he took you home."

*They must be close. How would she even know that?*

"I get it," Sherry said with a nod. "Don't answer. I get why."

"Do you still love him?" Amanda asked.

Sherry turned away and nodded. Then she squinted up against the sun over the truck walls again. The truck was so bumpy it was killing Amanda's side.

"Next stop," Sherry said, still trying to gaze over the metal wall. But she didn't dare sit up. "We make a run for it."

"I thought you said they'll gun us down?"

"Do we have a choice? I'll tape your mouth back and you can just hold your hands together. Then I'll jump out and scream and holler to get lots of attention. While they're chasing me, you can quietly run."

"No way. I'm not letting you take the fall."

"One of us has to, Amanda."

She reached for Amanda's face. Amanda turned. "I'll tape you and you'll pretend to still be tied. I'll make such a fuss that it will distract them from you."

"No." Amanda batted her hand away. "I won't let you sacrifice yourself."

"Don't fight me!"

"I won't," Amanda said, shaking her head. "We either both run or we don't go at all."

Sherry reached for her face again. Amanda hit her arm.

Sherry tackled her, trying to pin her. Amanda elbowed the old woman in the ribs. Then she butted her head against hers. It hurt...*real* bad. They both groaned.

Amanda thought that was it. But then Sherry leaped at her again, threw her against the wall of the truck, and pinned her, trying to press the tape against her lips. Amanda couldn't believe they were in a fight. The oddest thing was Sherry was trying not to make any noise. Worse, this was her way of helping her!

That gave Amanda an idea. Amanda cried out as loud as she could.

"*Fuck!*" Sherry said in a forced whisper. "*Shut the hell up! You idiot!*"

"Let go of me or I'll make more noise," Amanda warned.

Sherry rolled back toward the other side of the truck. She ran her hand through her long gray hair and rolled her eyes. Then she sat there panting. "You don't get it. Only one of us can get out of here. Whatever good you think you're doing."

"Both of us or neither," Amanda said, shaking her head.

Sherry looked up, more worried than ever, after Amanda's shout. But there was still the same rush of air with the occasional revving of the surrounding bikes. Sherry shrugged. "We can both die then."

"Fine. Just don't ever touch me like that again."

"Hmm," Sherry quipped with a smirk, staring at Amanda. "Well, keep your guard up, young-me, or I'll tie you up yet."

"Why don't we work together instead?"

Sherry looked up at the sky again, worried as hell. Then she shook her head. "I should have left you tied."

Amanda's eyes wandered around the truck bed. She was beginning to hate her twin. She'd look anywhere but at her. But eventually her eyes fell back on Sherry's face. She was surprised to see that same reassuring rueful grin she had glimpsed when she first landed in the truck. Sherry was nice as hell. Sherry wasn't fighting to hurt her, she was fighting to save her life.

Well, Amanda wouldn't let her. "Together," Amanda insisted.

Sherry looked away. She hesitantly nodded.

**33**

---

# RED OR BLACK

THE TIRES SCREECHED AND THE TRUCK LURCHED TO THE side. The turn was so violent that it rolled Sherry over Amanda. Then Amanda felt the cabin shimmy back and forth, struggling to maintain control. At one point, she felt like she was going to be launched over the wall. There was shouting. It wasn't just her screams. Then there was gunfire.

"Stay down!" Sherry said.

The floor swerved again, turning very sharply and pressing her against the wall of the truck. A biker rode so close that Amanda could see his helmet. He was looking in.

Amanda was dying to get up and see what was going on, but Sherry kept pressing her body down.

"Are we just going to stay inside?" shouted Amanda.

More gunshots. They came so close that Amanda covered her head. So did Sherry. And the truck wasn't slowing down—it felt like it was speeding up.

Sherry rose onto her knees and looked outside.

*What a hypocrite!*

"John!" Sherry shouted. "John!"

More bullets, this time hitting the inside of the truck. A

few stray shots bounced inside the cabin. And this time, Amanda was the one to yank Sherry back down.

"I thought you said to stay down!" Amanda said.

"Couldn't resist," Sherry said with a shrug. "Sorry."

"How far is—"

One of the motorcyclists leaped inside the truck bed. He managed to land right on Amanda's left leg, blinding her with pain for a moment. Then he reached for Sherry. As he leaned down to grab her, he was thrown against the front of the truck bed. His helmet cracked the small tinted window. Then his body was pelted by gunfire. He shook from bullets riddling his chest. Then the man, now quite dead, collapsed over them.

"How far is he from us?" cried Amanda.

"He's right behind us."

"How does he even know we're here?"

"We're the only car in the pack."

Her leg stung and hurt like hell. Sherry rose to her knees and shoved the fallen man off them. Then, gruesomely, she pushed him to the wall and over the side.

More shots quickly got her to duck again.

"Should we jump?" Amanda asked.

"We're driving a hundred miles an hour."

"Then what do we do?"

Sherry didn't have time to answer. They were both rammed hard against the front of the truck and then rolled over each other again. The truck was turning sharply. She wondered what was going on. Were they turning around at a break in the divider on the highway? It felt like that.

No. They were slowing down. Maybe she could jump out now? But before she could rise, the side of the truck was hit. She heard a squeal and felt the truck unnaturally drag sideways. For a second, she feared it would flip over. That would kill them for sure.

"He's ramming us!" Sherry said.

The truck slid sideways across the road and came to a standstill. Sherry tugged Amanda up. Amanda could now witness the mayhem. It wasn't just the biker gang surrounding them, she was surprised to see—though it was early in the morning with light traffic. Cars were strewn all over the highway, many overturned, others on their sides, some even aflame. And behind the cavalcade of black bikes were police cars. Red and blue was flashing behind the field of overturned cars.

Amanda recognized their location from a quick glance at a hill. White windmills. That meant they were near Palm Springs. All of this was processed in seconds because Sherry and Amanda were ducking bullets again.

John swung open his car and started shooting like crazy at the nearby bikes. Sherry helped Amanda off the pickup. Amanda landed, hampered by her injured leg, in a low crouched position. Then she groaned due to the pain in her leg. She found herself limping toward John's car despite the gunfire. Sherry was beside her.

Sherry threw the passenger door of John's car open and helped Amanda get in. Then John shut his driver's side door. That's when, aside from stray bullets cracking and intense pain, Amanda suddenly remembered in horror that John's car had only two seats.

*"No!"*

But Sherry had already shut the door. Amanda cried out for Sherry—she'd have her sit on top of her if she had to—but it was too late. Through the side mirror, Amanda saw a biker grab Sherry. She recognized that dreaded white scarf. It was their ringleader, Samael. Then, oddly, the other bikers started tying Sherry to the back of his motorcycle with rope.

Amanda was thrown against the seat as the car accelerated forward.

"John, we have to go back!" Amanda cried. "We have to go back for Sherry!"

John stared ahead, deadpan. Emotionless.

"John! Go back! We have to save her!"

But he wasn't ignoring her. He was turning the car around on the opposite side of the highway. A police officer barreled forward and slammed into the passenger side. John quickly turned his wheel and rammed the police car out of his way. Then they came about an inch from a head-long collision with a disabled truck.

Sherry sat behind Samael, roped to him and his motor-cycle as Samael re-entered the highway.

"Open the glove compartment and put your shades on," John said.

Amanda quickly pressed the glove compartment button and snatched her shades.

"And put your fucking seat belt on."

"I'm sorry, John."

He furrowed his brow and glanced at her. Then he looked down at her pants and up at her shirt. "Are you hurt?"

She shook her head. She wasn't going to tell him about her leg. She didn't care right now. He nodded and gazed forward. Then he continued to mow down any black bike in his way, while swerving around innocent trucks and cars, heading for Samael. But the demon finally took off like a flash of light between two cars. Multicolored light gathered across John's windshield as Amanda was pushed back in her seat during the pursuit.

"Where…" she muttered. "Do you know where Samael's taking her?"

"Los Angeles."

**34**

---

# THEIR MORNING COMMUTE

The relief of being safe in John's super car soon transformed into sheer terror. There were constant collisions with fenders and doors, horns honking, people shouting. It reminded Amanda of bumper cars, as metallic objects crashed and slid along the passenger side window. John was chasing the motorcycle gang. Samael, with his white scarf and Sherry behind him, was front and center, leading the pack. But zooming around cars was not as bad as the flashes of light. Every time the bikers zoomed into rays of light, she was thrown back in her seat and, even with sunglasses, burned by the bright light. And the obstacles were only getting harder to dodge. Some vehicles ricocheted off John's car and went spinning out of control. Then came bullets raining down from the bikers shooting at them. Tragically, a few stray shots hit bystanders' windshields. One windshield was splashed with red.

John kept looking up at the sky. She didn't understand why, until she spotted a helicopter and copter-like black objects overhead. The squad cars couldn't possibly catch up, and even when they did, the bikers simply rammed them out of the chase. Not so with the objects in the sky. The sky ahead teemed with more and more black flying machines. And even with the jumps in speed, these pursuers could keep up with them.

"What are they doing?" Amanda asked.

He didn't answer. Instead, he tapped hard on the car console. He scrolled down to a contact named "Hunter."

"Rick was shot, John."

John avoided hitting a flipped big rig on the highway. He squeezed through smoky bent metal. The car shook, running over debris. Many cars were pulling over on the shoulder. But even with people trying to avoid the violence, traffic was thickening.

The phone rang. And rang.

"He was shot, John," Amanda repeated quietly.

"Yeah," said a man warily on the other end of the phone line.

"I need support now," John said.

"Are you okay, Rick?" Amanda cried, staring at the console.

"No… " Rick said on the other line. "And no…John. I'm lying on the fucking floor."

"Put me in contact with someone who can, then," John said.

"Fuck, that asshole hit me in the back." He groaned. "What a cheap shot. Sounds like you have her with you now. Is that Amanda? Or Sherry?"

"Amanda," she said.

"Well, isn't that enough? Turn around and give up the chase."

"I need support now." John looked up at the sky. "If you can't do it, send me their number and I'll call them off." Amanda glanced in her side mirror. Red and blue lights were flashing. This time, it was a whole army of police. But the police were busy dodging obstacles on the highway left by the collisions too. John didn't seem to care. He kept looking up at the sky.

In the distance, Amanda caught the LA skyline. But seeing all those high rises now was bizarre. They had just been in Palm Springs, normally two hours away.

"They won't listen to you even if I give it," Rick muttered.

"They're tearing up the city. Before you die, call in support."

"You're such an asshole, John," Rick said. "What do you see in him, Amanda?"

"I'll call an ambulance to the café," Amanda said. She wasn't sure why she hadn't before.

*Because you were in the middle of a chase with devils.*

"Look out, John!" cried Amanda.

They rammed right into two cars. At their speed, both cars were hurled into the sides of his car. In front of him, Samael slammed on the brakes. John didn't stop. His car rammed into him, pinning Sherry. Amanda screamed. But somehow, after Samael rode ahead, Sherry didn't even seem to have been touched by the impact. The police fell back. Samael's slamming on his brakes had worked.

Then the demon took off again, speeding along the shoulder of the highway. John followed right behind. There were less police but now, up ahead, there was a line of red lights: cars motionless in traffic.

"Rick?" John asked. There was no response. "Rick!"

"Shit," John said. He hit his steering wheel and pressed a button, hanging up the phone.

"This is it," John said, gesturing to the traffic. He took a deep breath. "They have to stop. They won't get through that line of cars."

There was an accident blocking traffic on the freeway.

Even the shoulders were blocked. The median was too narrow for a motorcycle. And police were directing all the jammed cars into an immobile line of cars along the right shoulder, John and the gang's frequent escape route.

Samael gave a few hand signals to his biker gang. Then, instead of braking, he sped up toward the red lights. All the gang's motorcycles turned into a blur of light running headlong into the stalled traffic. The impact at this speed was as if a fiery bowling ball had been thrown down the center of the highway. Cars were thrown high in the air, and others were torn in half or exploded. It was so destructive that the damage tunneled a corridor of mangled and fiery broken metal through the center of traffic.

"*Jesus!*" John exclaimed.

Amanda was thrown forward against her belt as John slammed on the brakes. He stopped right at the entrance of the demon corridor.

People were jumping out of their cars. One woman was bleeding, trying to force the back door of her SUV open. Her poor kids were banging on the windows. And her face was covered in blood. Then an explosion erupted from another auto with a man standing by it. The fire raged and engulfed him in flames. Amanda could hear cries of others nearby, despite the quiet insulation of John's super car.

"Why are you stopping?" Amanda asked. "What's wrong?" She gestured at the fiery corridor. "Go chase after them."

"The car can't fit."

"Make it wider. Push the cars to the side."

"I can't do that, Amanda."

"Why?"

This was so weird. It was quiet in his soundproof car with just the occasional muffled scream. But they were surrounded by smoke, fire, and rubble. She felt like she was parked before a battle scene.

Meanwhile, the red and blue lights were getting bright in her side mirror. She was going to be arrested again.

"Why not, John?" Amanda repeated more quietly.

He didn't answer. He just sat staring from behind his shades at the narrow corridor.

Far in the distance now, another car was thrown airborne. The bikes were still plowing through cars miles ahead.

"You care about these people? Is that it?" she asked, staring at him. It seemed like such a simple question, but she felt like it meant the whole world. "You're not bad, John," she said, shaking her head. "You're good."

He finally turned and stared at her. Then he wrapped his arm around the back of her seat, turned, and looked out the back window.

"I'm not good."

She was thrown toward the door and then the windshield. Her seat belt was the only thing keeping her in her seat as John raced backward through oncoming traffic. At first, it was thick. But after another half mile, it thinned out. The police had cleared a lot of the highway.

He rushed by the army of police cars. One slid past the passenger door. The siren blared in her ears as the squad car was hit and rammed into a nearby truck. Then came a swarm of more red and blue rushing by the windows. Another was hit on John's side. But most swerved out of his way. None of it stopped him. But it seemed like, unlike the bikers, he was doing everything he could to avoid the cars on the road.

After passing the police, he continued driving backward at over a hundred miles an hour. Stray cars, many turned over by the earlier violence, now flew by the window. She couldn't believe John could maneuver like this.

"I think I'm going to be sick," Amanda said.

She pressed the window switch and rolled down the

window. As she was tossed back and forth in her seat, she grasped for the handlebar above. Clutching it, she vomited on whatever passed by. After a few more heaves, breathing heavily, she sat back and put her head in her hands. She noticed car horns and shouting, police sirens, and a rush of wind from the now open window.

John shut her window.

"Are you all right?" he asked, glancing over.

"I think some of it came in," Amanda said. "I'm sorry."

She couldn't believe he was still racing backward.

Mercifully, the path soon straightened. Then he seemed to hug the median.

"I don't care about the fucking car," John said. "Are you okay, Mandi? Are you all right?"

She quietly nodded, wiping her mouth. Then she said very quietly, more to herself, "I really love you."

The route became mercifully straight.

Police cars, with their red and blue lights flashing, were heading straight at them now, or behind them, but they still couldn't stop his car. A few tried to ram the sides, but that just led to more crashing. Even a few stray bullets bounced off the glass.

"Hold on," John said.

*Shit, that doesn't sound good.*

She was thrown against the door as John turned and drove through an opening in the median. The car drifted a hundred and eighty degrees onto the other side of the freeway. They missed the concrete median by inches. As John straightened, his car nearly came to a standstill. Then they were launched forward again. This time, thankfully, driving on the right side of the freeway.

John touched the console. He started searching maps. Then he touched another button, causing a phone to ring.

"Where are you going?" she asked.

"Away from the city."

"That will be away from Sherry." *Shut up, Mandi. He knows that.*

He worked the console again. Then he leaned forward and looked up at the sky .

"What's up there?" Amanda asked.

"I'm waiting for them to hit us," he said, staring at the machines above. "That's why we have to run."

"Hit us? With what?"

"Bombs. After what they just did, it's just a matter of time before they knock us all off the road."

"Will the car survive?"

He shook his head.

Traffic got worse. She realized it must be because they had passed the area the police had cleared. But now they were entering morning traffic. And every time he had a long opening, he did that irritating blinding-light-exploding thing.

Then Amanda caught an explosion in her rearview mirror. It looked like a plume of smoke but it seemed so far away.

"That them?" Amanda asked.

He nodded.

The phone just kept ringing.

Then John hit his steering wheel. He started searching the maps while passing more cars. Amanda gazed at the speedometer. She wished she hadn't. It read one hundred and eighty. He was driving at that speed while flipping through maps again.

"Something I can do to help?" she said.

He stopped on a map with a red dot.

"What are you doing?" Amanda asked. She almost didn't want to ask.

"Trying to track that explosion."

"So, if one of those bombs hits her—"

"She dies."

"So does Samael."

"I don't care about Samael, Sherry."

"Amanda," she corrected, though quietly. "Amanda. My name's Amanda, John."

Another red dot beeped on the map. Then a yellow one.

"That them?" she asked.

"That's another explosion."

"The yellow?"

"That's them jumping."

"So we can find them."

He nodded. "We can track them." Then he looked up. "Maybe Rick did help us. They haven't fired on us yet."

"John, it looks like this yellow dot is further from downtown." She leaned forward and spread her fingers on the screen. John was about to grab her, but she managed to enlarge the area on the map. "He's leaving LA and heading back out. Look, this area of the map reads 'Pasadena'."

"His plan to lure me failed. Now he's running, like us. But he still wants to lure me. He knows we will follow if—"

The car tires suddenly squealed as he turned the wheel so sharply it threw Amanda against the door. Then in a split second she was thrown back just as hard. She felt intense pain from the seat belt. John had avoided hitting a stalled vehicle on the shoulder. His super car quickly corrected, moving straight as if nothing had happened.

"I think they haven't shot us down yet," he said, ignoring the near collision, "because we're leaving. I don't think Rick did a thing."

"He was shot, John." *Why do you keep telling him that?*

"I know, *Amanda*," he said with a quick glance at her and a rare smile. He stared at her for a moment. She smiled.

"The morning traffic's only getting worse," he said. "Hopefully, you're right and they're leaving LA."

"Can we slow down, then?" *Please!* He didn't answer. She really didn't expect him to. So she asked something else on her mind. "Has it ever gotten this bad?"

He shook his head.

## 35

## ANGELS DOWN

They rushed through a nauseating ordeal of high, rolling hills. They zoomed so fast it seemed the car was leaping over them. Then, at their immense speed, the flat desert sand, bushes, and weeds rapidly sprawled out before them for as far as the eye could see. The hills were gone. And so, again, she was out in that infinite horizon she loved. The sky was clear. The sun was out. If she hadn't been stuck in the middle of a car chase, it could have been beautiful. Only it wasn't a view to enjoy right now.

Because John wasn't slowing down. He was rapidly closing in on his target, following that yellow light on his monitor.

"We've almost caught up," John said. He'd been quiet ever since passing Palm Springs again. He pointed at another yellow dot that had just appeared on the map. It looked close to the center. "The car's faster than the motorcycles."

"But why's he taking her into the desert?" asked Amanda. "I thought he wanted you in the city?"

John pointed up. Pitch-black machines were hovering overhead. "He wants me dead. He doesn't care how."

"Why weren't those black things popping up before?"

"They were probably hoping the police could handle the chase."

"Those aren't the police?"

He shook his head. "He'll probably either disappear jumping full speed," John added, studying the map on the console again, "or give up and turn around."

"What do you mean *full speed*?"

*That doesn't sound good.*

John abruptly turned the wheel ever so slightly, just an inch. If he hadn't, they would have driven through a truck. At this speed, it took only slight shifting of the wheel to avoid obstacles. He was constantly doing it, even while talking. But it seemed like the car helped him. There were times when it looked like he needed to turn more sharply and the car corrected his steering.

A very small metallic flying object rushed right by Amanda's window. With metallic wings, it reminded her of a bug.

"There's little hope for Sherry," John said, gazing at the object in his rearview mirror. "Just like there was little hope when they marked your friend Luane."

"Or me," Amanda said, touching his arm. "But you saved me."

"Well, I should drop you off now."

Amanda looked at the clock on the console. It read 9:40. During their chase through hell, it had been a little before eight. How? Then in Palm Springs she thought it read a little after eight-fifteen. That was so weird.

"Well, I'm not leaving, John. I'm not leaving until we help her."

"Amanda," he said, glancing at her. "How are you helping her? You didn't come for her, you came for me."

"No, I came for my interview." She gave a nervous chuckle.

"You came for me. That was stupid. All that did was bring you into danger again. I told you to stay in LA. You're still marked."

"Well, I really do have an interview."

"Your friend just died and—"

"Luane's alive," Amanda snapped. "Okay. She didn't die. She's in the hospital."

"Oh…" he looked at her and furrowed his brow for a moment. She felt the car quickly sway to the left and saw a car blur across her passenger window. "Good. Then you should be caring for her, not chasing cars on the highway with me."

"Well, yeah, Lu's alive. And her getting shot was my fault. So? I get all that. Her danger, I get, was on me. But my danger's my business." She folded her arms. "Anyway, seems like this devil is leading you to where I was going anyway. *My interview*, John. It's in Phoenix. We're on Interstate Ten. So it all works out real convenient."

He frowned. "Next rest stop, I'm dropping you off."

"The fuck you are." She flapped a finger at the map. "You… you…you drop me off and she'll be long gone."

He fell silent. Because she was right. All she heard was the constant hum of the engine, like being on an airplane.

He took a deep breath while staring at the road.

She scooted back and threw her feet up on the dash. "Afraid you're stuck with me. Till you get me to my interview. It's in Scottsdale, by the way. Just a quick one-second detour for your rocket car. This seat is more comfortable than an airplane, anyway. I'll just scoot back, let you do your demon chase shit, enjoy the view, and wait to help you get back your older me. Your older-*Amanda*, John. Amanda. Not Sherry."

She winked at him. He laughed. That made her laugh too.

But then the smile she loved vanished from his face. She

was thrown against her seat again. It took a few seconds to figure out why they were racing faster. John had found his prey.

She saw only two black bikes now, each taking up one lane in front of them. Had the rest been destroyed?

The demon still held Sherry on his back. He was riding in the right lane; the other biker was in the left. She could tell it was Sherry by her long gray hair. She wasn't wearing a helmet. But she didn't look back because her head crouched tightly into the beast's back. Amanda shuddered imagining what it must feel like for poor Sherry zooming at these incredible speeds on a motorcycle just hanging on to his back.

The other black-clad biker looked back. Then he dropped back by the driver's side of the car, took out some sort of club, and swung it at the window. He missed. And that made him lose control of his bike. He spun onto the opposite side of the highway.

John drove right up to Samael's motorcycle, nearly touching Samael and Sherry.

"Be careful," Amanda cried.

She fell back in her seat as he accelerated right into them. Amanda screamed.

"She's protected by the bike," John said.

He was right. She hadn't been harmed. But the bike headed toward the shoulder.

"But she'll fall off!"

*He knows. He knows.*

Amanda flew forward again, feeling pain in her chest from the belt as John slammed on the brakes. Samael stopped too. Sand kicked up and covered the windows. Amanda wasn't sure why they had both come to a complete stop. Until she saw this huge black flying machine with bright lights hovering over Samael's bike and their car. It reminded her of a UFO. There were some words from a megaphone. But as Samael skidded his bike along the freeway, swerving around the huge metallic onyx structure, John rocketed forward chasing him. And whatever words were being said by the flying machine, the sound stretched and faded as the chase resumed.

When the freeway horizon became flat, Samael's bike blurred. Amanda was pressed against her seat again. At this speed, the valleys and turns rushed by faster than Amanda had ever seen.

Amanda was thrown against her passenger door by a sudden turn. John was avoiding wreckage from a semitruck that had been torn in half by the impact of Samael's bike. Then the other biker, the one that had spun out off the freeway, appeared again. It rode through the wreckage but then collided with a van up ahead.

There was an explosion. Sand and dirt blew over their windshield. Amanda felt the car bounce over rough road, and dust covered her window. Her ears rang from the noise. Then there was a plume of sand in the desert off to the side. And another geyser exploded right by her window. As she looked in her rearview mirror, desert sand mixed with flames lighting the dust as more explosions engulfed the highway behind them. Soon dust filled the sky and occluded the sun, making it dark.

John swerved around an SUV.

Another blast exploded ahead. This one rattled Samael's bike. The bike shook and looked like it was going to turn sideways. Samael recovered. Then he blurred into lights again, moving faster than ever. Way faster. John was losing them.

"We have to stop this now," John said. He searched the sky.

Far into the dusty sky Amanda spotted another black object.

"Hold on."

*Oh, no. Not again.*

John sped the car up even faster. The dust quickly cleared and the blue sky was suddenly completely clear. But mountains and valleys now passed her like cars. And in the midst of the mayhem, she wasn't sure why, she gazed down at the console. Then she stared at it. The digital clock read 3:45 in the afternoon. How! A few seconds later, it read 4:11. It had been nine in the morning just a minute ago.

A bridge that looked miles ahead blurred by in seconds. In the sunlight it was a quick flicker. At this speed, hills moved like cars, but the copter bombing stopped. They must have lost them. So why hadn't Samael done this before?

But then, even more oddly, the bike chase slowed. The colored lights faded. John's speedometer quickly dropped to only one-hundred-and-ninety miles an hour.

Samael was slowing down. Then, and this was really bizarre, Samael reached back with a knife and started cutting the ropes holding Sherry behind him. John gripped the wheel and his jaw clenched.

John rammed them. Samael was thrown like a cue ball, shimmying along the desert highway. But he recovered. Then he was back to cutting ropes behind him.

"Oh, no," Amanda said.

Sherry down, indeed. Samael was cutting her to let her go. Without a helmet and at this speed, Sherry would just die. And the devil wanted John to see it, just as Lilith had wanted her to see her friend shot in the head on the bridge.

The only thing merciful was the lack of traffic on the highway. But this was weird because more buildings were cropping up. It seemed like they were now approaching Phoenix.

Amanda saw a red streak appear by the driver's side window.

John's phone rang. The contact read "Hunter."

"Fall back, John," Rick said weakly on the car speakers. "Now. This is enough."

"She'll die if you knock him off," John said. "If you kill him now, she'll die."

"She's dead anyway. Fall back."

"No." John looked up again, searching the skies. "Tell them to leave."

A rope was cut. That left just one more holding Sherry to the bike. She clung to her jailor's back more tightly than ever. Her whole body now twisted and turned on the bike, struggling to stay on. John sped to the right shoulder and moved in front of Samael, slamming on the brakes. Samael simply swerved, now with Sherry barely holding on. John fell behind him again.

"She's gone," Rick said. "Forget it. Look up."

Amanda crouched forward and looked through the windshield. There seemed to be a swarm of black flying machines above.

"We're all dead anyway, then," John said.

"They won't let him get to Phoenix," Rick said. "After everything that happened in LA, they're not gonna let it go on today. I came to stop them from shooting you down. Now fall back, John. Fall back so you and Amanda don't die too."

Samael cut the last rope. Sherry's body was flapping against his bike. She was clutching as best she could to her kidnapper. The only thing allowing her to stay on was their slowing speed.

A bomb fell. This time it landed right in front of Samael. It forced him to swerve his bike, skidding along the road almost to a stop.

*"Fall back now! Now, John!"*

Amanda saw Rick's car grind to a halt, and his red car rushed backward.

Amanda was flung forward against her seat belt. There

was a flash of light. Then she was thrown to the side. Then came a gust of wind and smoke against all the windows. Amanda felt the car spin, turn over, and start rolling. The earth and sky seemed to switch positions. Gusts of smoke and dirt covered the glass, but she saw the ground. It was flipping repeatedly around her. The car was rolling. Then more dust and smoke filled the windows until it grew dark. And then…silence.

She looked over at John. Behind him, through a dusty window, she saw the sky below them. The car was turned over upside down. He was closing his eyes tight. His shades were on the floor—or the ceiling. He looked unharmed. She looked at herself. No scratch on her either. And the car? There wasn't even a dent and the glass hadn't even cracked.

"Are you okay?" he asked.

For the first time in the chase, without the sunglasses, she saw his eyes. There was water around those bags. And his angel eyes were bloodshot. Behind his shades, he had been crying.

"Are you all right, Amanda? Amanda? Are you okay?"

Amanda couldn't answer.

John threw off his seat belt, curled up in a ball, and fell to the ground-ceiling. Then he threw the door open. She watched him, backward. He put a hand over his forehead and stared through the dirt and smoke. He stood there for the longest time, just staring, until the cloud of dust cleared. He was motionless, staring with naked eyes because…

*Sherry was dead.*

**36**

---

# HE JUST NODDED

JOHN DROVE AMANDA HOME. AFTER A CREW OF HIS SECRET police friends in black heaved his super car over, he just drove her home. Initially, he had gotten back on the highway and driven toward Phoenix, but then, per Amanda's request—the only time she said anything—he turned his car around. He was actually still going to take her to Scottsdale despite everything that had happened. She had just said three words. "Take me home."

She had never come for the interview. John had been right. She had come for him. Now solemn as hell, her guardian weirdly drove the speed of traffic on the freeway. That was so strange. But no one driving by thought anything was amiss. His car was filthy though, caked in dust. But there wasn't even a scratch.

Heading back to LA, he veered south and soon merged with Interstate Eight. She nodded to herself at that coincidence. This was near the place they had met.

She had seen his tears. But now, after finding his shades in the wreck, he was his usual self. Probably more so. Deadpan. Opaque.

"Rick said..." She was surprised at how loud her voice seemed. "He said you were going to ascend, but instead you came back for her. Why?"

He was fixed on the highway and didn't even turn. She expected to see him clench the wheel, the way she had seen him do so many times before when upset. He didn't. He just drove.

"Why? Why'd you do that, John? When you knew...she wouldn't make it?"

"I didn't know it would be Sherry. I thought it could be you."

She nodded and stared out the window. A car drove by along the desert freeway. Just a lady wearing sunglasses driving her white SUV on the freeway. Two kids were sitting in the back. Nothing special. They were just normal people driving on the highway.

*That's what people do, right?*

"I had to try," he added.

She squeezed his right hand, which was leaning on the arm rest. "I'm sorry."

"When you take me back," she said, shaking her long hair back, "you don't have to give me your number. Just take me home. Take me back to my friend Luane. You were right. I need to take care of my friend."

His eyebrows furrowed. But then he just nodded.

And then she cried. She turned to the car door, rolled up in a ball, stared at the infinite horizon of sands and weeds she so adored, and faced them. And just cried. She hated herself for it; the last thing she wanted was his sympathy, so she faced the window. But she couldn't stop. And she cried for him because she knew he wouldn't.

"I'm...sorry," she said. "I'm so sorry."

More silence. All she heard was the rumble of the engine.

"I'll give you my number," he said.

"I don't care, John. I'm not crying about that. I'm crying for you and Sherry."

He just nodded.

**37**

---

# DONE WITH ROAD TRIPS

L*UANE SLOWLY OPENED AN EYELID A CRACK AS* A*MANDA LAID* a small cactus on a table beside her bed. She intended to just sit in a recliner and let her sleep, but her friend stirred. Then she groaned. She had all those wires out of her face, but she still looked awful. And there was still a plastic wire connected to her arm.

It was bright in the room. The sun shone through the window.

Luane turned and gave a faint smile. "You're back. How'd your interview go, babe?"

"It didn't."

"Huh?" She opened her eyes wider. She tried to sit up, and Amanda rushed over to help her.

"Don't worry about me."

"What happened?"

"Got into a car accident."

"Another one! Oh my God, are you okay, Mands?"

"I'm fine." Amanda nodded. Then she pulled up a chair and sat down. "Don't worry. I finally got you a cactus." She forced a smile. "This one's from a gas station. The first one was so easy to come by, I don't know why.

Now I had to get you this replacement. Anyway, while you don't have any men warming you, the spikes can remind you of Ben."

"Bitch," she said with a smile. "What happened, babe? You were so looking forward to your interview. Are you all right?"

"I'm fine. There'll be others. I told them what happened and they'll see if they can accommodate, but they've already rescheduled, you know. Anyway, don't worry, Lu. I wanted to come back for you. You're most important."

She squeezed Luane's hand and smiled again. But she couldn't help but feel like her grin was fake. She felt nothing happy about seeing her friend like this. Or thinking of everything that had happened.

"The doctor said you won't be here much longer," Amanda said. "And when you go home, you're gonna need someone to help you around our place."

Luane patted Amanda's hand.

"I love ya, babe," Lu said, nodding. "But I'll be able to take care of myself. Did you check our mail? Any news for me?"

"Nothing more yet."

"Maybe I'll get lucky like you. I just hope if I land one, it's nearby and not across the country. I don't want to go anywhere near a freeway after everything you've been telling me about."

"Me neither," Amanda said, dropping back into her chair. "I'm so done with road trips."

**38**

---

# THE MAN WITH NO NAME

"WELL, WHAT CAN I SAY, GUYS? I'M AT IT AGAIN. ANOTHER road trip." Amanda laughed. "You know Caligirl gettingold24 could only stay home for so long, guys. I fucking love the open road. Just now, I passed the familiar buildings of the Los Angeles skyline, heading into the empty highway, where the only company is an occasional ground squirrel or bird fluttering in the sparse bushes and trees. Not like home. No mountains, skyscrapers, or beachy sand. Actually, we just passed *a lot* of sand. I wanted to slide down it, it was a dune like snow, but grumpy wasn't in the mood.

"It's desolate as hell out here, and… I absolutely adore that. You know I'm freaky like that. Oh look. I just passed a tree. That was like the only tree for four miles, guys.

"How can I describe to you what I'm seeing? Let's give it a try… There's an ugly cream-colored one-story building with a red roof behind a gate. It's not long, so hold on a minute… There. It's gone. Now I'm rushing by a fence, and beyond are fluffy bushes scattered along dirt. Lots of that. These mangy dog-hairs along the sand are everywhere. Just scattered bushes like a mangy dog. I absolutely adore it.

"Here's what else I love. Comments to my show. I've got to thank my listeners..." She tore her eyes from the passenger window and reached into a pocket. She unfolded a sheet of paper. "DirkyJ. You said I have a sweet voice. You said you listen every time for a new show. Thanks, Dirk! Or Dirky. I'm so happy when one of my listeners likes my show. Jerrybutt12 said I'm a lot of fun. Well, I'm really not. But I like to talk a whole lot. I'm kinda boring, really—sans the death-defying road trips. Brittany501 said she loved the story about that shadow man in Colorado. She asked, "Did you find that shadow man again in Arizona?" Well, as a matter of fact—"

John turned from the road and stared at her through his shades. She held the microphone toward him. He shook his head.

Then she pushed her note back into her jeans pocket, undid her lap belt, threw her feet up on the dash, and laughed. When John turned but didn't say anything —'cause she knew he'd die if he was recorded—she laughed even harder.

"I haven't got my car back yet, you know, Brittany. It's still in a parking lot in Cincinnati. But, you know, someone had to drive me to my interview. Yeah, they rescheduled me. How fucking amazingly great is that? Right! And you guys know Luane is still recovering at home. Thank God, she's feeling better. So a lot of stuff is going well. But my new rental was totally totaled. So, how's a girl supposed to get to Phoenix? Hmm…John? What do you think?"

And he glared at her. "Erase that."

She clicked her recorder off and frowned.

"And put your seat belt on."

"No."

"You know you can't have people know about me," he

said, staring back at the road. They were driving at a "normal" speed. That's why she had dared to take her seat belt off. Well that, and because she knew she could get a rise out of him.

"I told you in New York I don't like being told what to do," Amanda said.

"I'm not telling you what to do. This is for your safety."

"It's my life."

"Well, unveiling my name—"

"John, do you have any idea how many people are named John?"

"You can be so irritating," he said, shaking his head.

"Not as irritating as Sherry, I bet?"

*Oops. That was so stupid. Why mention her? Idiot!*

"I didn't mean that, John. Sorry."

"Just put your belt on," he said. And he actually smiled. "Actually, you're acting just like her. If anything, that's annoying me more."

"It still hurts. I know. Sorry." She rubbed his hand. "You sure you're up to stopping by her place?"

"I don't like the fact that no one's been looking after it. And it's really not her place. It's ours. It's owned under my name. I let her run it. I was happy for her to keep it and run it for us. She named the place, you know. It's called Angel Dive."

"Angel Dive?" Amanda said with a guffaw. "Are you joking? Angel Dive? That is so funny!"

He shook his head.

"That's really good," she said. "I love it. I love it a lot. It's funny, but true. *Angel Dive.*"

"Sherry was good with words like you, Amanda. You two were a lot alike. A bit too alike."

"So…" Amanda turned back to the window and stared at those bushes she'd called "soft" to her listeners. They weren't soft. They were soft from a distance but thorny as hell, like a cactus. Kind of the opposite of her lover. "So... You sure you're up to this? You could just drive North to Scottsdale and forget about it."

"If you're willing, I'd rather make a quick stop, Mandi. You and Rick said the place was a mess."

"I don't mind at all," she lied. She kept having images of Samael flash in her mind.

She kicked her feet over the dash again. One foot touched John's windshield. Of course, the inside of his car was immaculate and he noticed.

"Put your seat belt on," he said.

She fell back in the car seat. "Sorry. Didn't mean to touch your precious—"

"Forget it. Put your belt on for your safety. And wear your shades, please."

She reached for her belt. But when she thought of sunglasses, she felt her hand shake. "You don't think I'll need sunglasses again?"

"You're marked. You'll be marked the rest of your life. Lilith's and Samael's vessels were destroyed, but they weren't. They'll be back, Amanda. I've killed them before. You can't kill evil. Unlike—"

He stopped talking and looked back at the road. She knew he was going to say *Sherry*. Then his hands gripped the wheel tight, like he used to when he was upset. She heard the click of her belt. She reached down for her bag, by her legs, and pulled out a pair of sunglasses. Then she rubbed John's arm again.

He went silent. John was always silent. Sometimes she hated it. Other times, she liked it, because it meant she was with him. Silence and mystery *was* John.

She pressed the play button of her small handheld recorder, hearing her voice... "*So, how's a girl supposed to get to Phoenix.*"

Click.

"There." She turned to him and said, "Erased."

"Thank you."

But she pressed record.

"What's his name. He's a man with no name. He doesn't want to be named, sorry. Nor does he want attention, unlike yours truly. He lurks in the shadows. Not scary, but in shadows. He's like a shade. To me, he's my protector. Anyway, I'm with him now, Brittany. Yeah. And I could never be happier.

"Brittany501, let me tell you 'bout him. He's..." She turned, studying him. "Dark, mysterious. He wears opaque sunglasses. You can't see behind them, like he's always trying to hide something. He's got on a matching black T-shirt and pants. Very dark. But he's got bulging muscles on his biceps." She laughed. "And strong pecs. Strong as hell. That's him. His hair is dark and short, but nicely groomed. Perfect. Handsome. His jaw and face are hard. He's got stubble. He's shaven, but he leaves it sort of unshaved across his face. And the five o'clock shadow is...perfect. But you can't see his eyes. You can't see them, and that's the greatest crime of all, even worse than the not-talking thing he does. Not blabbering is annoying enough to a girl like me, but not nearly as annoying as not looking into those eyes of his. He has the bluest, most lovely eyes on the planet. They're the opposite of his outer shell. They're the eyes of an angel."

Click.

*Damn, that's so good.*

"Amanda?"

"Yeah?" She took a big sigh. "What's up?"

"Erase that. That's worse than saying my name. You just described me."

She laughed. "God, I hate you, John."

He nodded and just kept driving.

"The hell I'm erasing that," she said. "No way. Sorry.

It's way too good. But…thanks again for taking me to my interview."

"You're welcome."

"And I'm kissing you the minute we stop the car."

"Suit yourself."

"I don't think you'd let me do it while you're on duty, mister. You know, on the road. I really want to, but I don't think you'll let me do it when you're driving. So I won't try now."

"You never know. You could try."

*Oh—okay.*

# 39

## ANGEL DIVE RETURN

As John turned into the parking lot, Amanda felt butterflies in her stomach. She didn't want to be here. She couldn't get images of that she-he devil out of her head. But she'd be there for John. She couldn't refuse him. He was driving her to her interview, after all. John seemed nervous too. She knew because she saw him gripping the wheel tightly again.

When he stopped the car in the dirt parking lot, she felt more dread than ever. The lot was vacant. Most of the windows were boarded up. And the roof on the left side was still charred from the fire. John sat for a moment and stared. Then he unlatched his belt, threw his car door open, as if he was fighting to get out, and came around the car to open the door for Amanda.

"Thanks," she said. He closed the door, staring again at the small one-story building.

He couldn't open the front door. So he heaved his shoulder into it. After a few crashes, the door flew open.

There was a gasp. It was Amanda's voice. The place was so clean. Not just clean, immaculate. Unlike last time, all the broken glass was gone. The walls were as she remembered, burgundy with pictures and silly stuff, but in perfect order. Nothing was damaged or even hung crooked. The empty stage was devoid of dust. And at the far end was the bar. In the dark, it was still charred, but all the glass had been taken off the counter and the floor had been swept. And all the wooden tables had the chairs turned over sitting neatly on them.

"What the hell," said a woman's voice behind the bar in the dark. "I'd love to know how the hell you got through that door. It's jammed. Anyway, scram. Place is closed." Then she gasped. "Oh my God. *John?*"

Amanda turned around and saw a light switch. She switched it on and the whole place lit up. And there Sherry stood, in a white T-shirt and jeans, behind the bar. But her wrinkled skin was parched and sunburned. Her eyes were bulging, staring at them.

She ran to him. They embraced tightly, kissing each other's lips.

"How are you here?" Amanda asked.

She looked at Amanda over his arms. It was so weird. It was as if Amanda were staring at herself in a mirror seeing John and herself in the future. She had the same long hair, but it was gray. Her skin was wrinkled. And with John's shades on, he could hide his age. It was exactly how she thought they'd look in a few decades.

"You brought him to me?" Sherry asked with a kind smile. "Thank you."

Amanda shook her head. Then she shut her mouth, realizing it was gaping open.

"How are you alive?" Amanda asked.

"After the explosion," she said, slowly moving out of John's embrace, "I was thrown from the bike."

"You didn't have a helmet."

"But the jerk slowed down to cut the ropes. Remember? I was traveling fast, but not fast enough. Apparently. I was thrown from the bike and away from the explosion. I mean, the accident was gnarly, but no broken bones."

"Rick didn't tell me," said John.

"He didn't know," Amanda said. Her voice echoed. It had been said at exactly the same time by Sherry. With the same voice.

"I figured you'd come by soon enough, John," Sherry said. "I was going to look for you, but you know you never gave me a way to contact you."

"I thought I was the only lucky girl with that problem," Amanda said.

"It's for safety," John explained to Amanda. Then he turned to Sherry. "Both of yours."

"Well, I've had time to get the place back in order," Sherry continued, looking around. Then everyone turned completely silent. They all looked at the diner together in uncomfortable silence.

"The place looks good, Sher," John finally said. He had lost his smile and Amanda almost laughed at his usual sternness.

"It damn well better," Sherry said, looking around again with a satisfied nod. "It took a lot of work. I don't know about the fire damage, though."

"I can get a crew to work on it," John said.

"Sure, John." Then Sherry gestured to Amanda. "Sure. Why's she here? I thought she was supposed to be safe in LA?"

"I have an interview," Amanda said.

Sherry squinted and nodded slowly.

Then there was more silence. And John, who had run into Sherry's embrace a second ago, was back to being Mr. Cool, standing back holding his hands in his jacket pockets. That almost made Amanda laugh.

"Let me have a word with her alone," Sherry said to

John. "Please." Sherry gently hugged John again and kissed his cheek. "I've missed you."

"Thank God you're all right," John said, patting her back. "I'll be outside."

The two of them watched John leave.

After he closed the broken door behind him, Amanda could just see his silhouette in the parking lot through a broken board in the window. He stood there, kicking dust with his boot and looking out on the horizon toward Yuma.

*Sherry's alive. So what does that mean for me?*

*Well, relationship is over, obviously, dummy.*

Amanda felt sluggish. Slow. The air seemed to weigh down on her.

"What will it be, young-me?" Sherry asked behind the bar counter.

"Huh?"

Sherry picked up an empty beer glass and smirked at Amanda.

"I made my place a bar, Amanda," she said. "I love talking to patrons, serving them drinks and just talking. I love this place. So, come on. This time, I'll have a drink and talk to you."

Amanda walked to the counter and sat on a stool. Everything still felt slow.

*Will we fight?*

"I'd like—"

"Wait," Sherry said, closing her eyes and raising a finger. "Let me guess. Cider. Right? That's your favorite?"

"Yeah."

"Mine too."

Sherry filled a glass at the tap.

As Amanda waited, she felt more uneasy. She was beginning to hate this place. Seeing herself was creepy enough, but feeling creepy reminded her of the last time she was in this dump with Rick and Samael. Maybe that's who this lady had been all along? What if she was going to change into Samael and then start shooting at them? She handed her a drink with a smile. *No, not with that sweet smile.*

"I've been thinking," Amanda said, sipping the drink, "you know, since the kidnapping, that I wished we could talk. I think I was more upset, when we thought we had lost you, at the possibility that it would never happen. I'm glad we can do that now."

"Me too." Sherry raised her glass. Amanda clinked it with hers. Sherry sipped the drink staring at Amanda. "Cheers. This is prime stuff. Organic, with a touch of cinnamon. Right off the tap."

Amanda drank and smiled back.

Sherry pointed to John in the parking lot. They both looked over.

"He loves you."

"No, he loves you."

"He loves you. When I awoke in the sand realizing I was alive, I had a lot of walking in the desert heat to do. I thought about you and him. And us. That's why I want to talk to you now before I go."

"Where are you going?"

"He sleeps on his side. Do him a favor, keep something under the bed to cushion his fall or at least yank him to the center. He falls off the bed all the time, Amanda. And he won't brush his teeth. I know, it's really gross, but he just won't do it. So every night, lay the toothbrush by the sink. Hell, even put the damn toothpaste on it. He'll be away a lot. But he'll care for you to death. And go get him a dog. A nice furry brown one. It's not only for him. He will fight you to hell and back again on getting a dog, but I tell you now, get him one. He doesn't know how much he loves them until he has them. Our favorite dog was named Bear."

"Why are you telling me all this?"

"He can't be with me. We tried. Maybe I'm too damned old. Or I'm too old to put up with his shit. But really, it wasn't the same. I mean we love each other, but not in a romantic way anymore. All he has is fleeting memories of our love. You're not. You and he are real."

Amanda shook her head.

"He's been in love with you ever since he met you," Sherry said. "I can tell from the way he talked about you. When I was young, I was rash, quick tempered, but energetic like you. Fun. Alive. I was you. You're what I've wanted for John all along since he's been back. You're what we lost. And, whatever you want to call it, whatever you say, young-me, the only arrangement that will work with a twenty-something man is you."

Amanda shook her head again, harder.

"Don't screw this up," Sherry said, sipping some cider. "Not if you love him as much as I do. He needs the young version of me. I'm a fleeting memory, you're real and now. And you don't only love him, he loves you. Me? I'm family. You, he's in love with you, Amanda."

"You can't keep sacrificing like this!" Amanda cried, jumping up from the stool. She surprised herself with her rage. "You and he keep doing this! That was the other thing I was going to say. You had no right to throw me in the car! He loves *you*. Not me. Look at the way you just kissed each other."

"Only one person could fit in his cursed car. I told you in my truck only one of us would make it. He didn't protect you across the country for nothing. He's not a nice guy, Amanda. He did it for you. Not me."

"Call me Mandi. And you know him far better than I do. You just told me all his secrets."

"Not all of them."

"I don't want this," Amanda snapped, shaking her head and pushing the drink across the counter. "I'm sorry, I'll let him drive me to my interview. Then I'm done. I can fly back home. He can come back to you."

"Who's sacrificing now?"

*Shit, we are fighting.*

But Sherry seemed to realize it too. She heaved a sigh, drank some cider, and looked away from Amanda, just staring at the empty stage. Then she nodded. Amanda stared at a red wall.

"Okay," Sherry finally said, "I'll try it another way. What interview are you going to, Mandi? Is it a job for a newspaper? I wanted to be a reporter too. I was working on that path right before I lost him."

"So?" Amanda put her hands on her hips, fuming.

Sherry frowned. Then she lifted an eyebrow and repeated, "So. We are the same person. And I think I know why."

"Yeah? Why?"

"Maybe I should get you another drink."

"Just tell me."

"Who's your parents?" Sherry asked.

"I was adopted."

Sherry shrugged.

"So?"

"Why don't you sit down?"

With the hand holding her drink, Sherry pointed outside, through cracks in the boards, at John. "John and I didn't connect only once after the accident. We connected twice. One time was shortly after he died—or I thought he had died. When he became an archangel. Did he tell you why he didn't see me until I'd aged so much?"

"Rick said something about it taking that long for him to return to Earth as an archangel."

Sherry shook her head. "It was instant. When he was first changed, I saw him a week or two later in LA. I had searched for him. I shouldn't have, but I did. Only he didn't remember who I was. It took a while for him to recall. The minute he changed, his past was erased. He had only fleeting memories, like he does now. So I did what you did. I hung out with him on my own little adventures. With his new position, like you, it put my life in jeopardy. Then I ended up on one of those cursed chases. In that damned magic car. And it was that cursed car that took my John from me."

"I don't understand."

"Do you know what happens when you travel fast?" Sherry asked. "I mean, really, really fast? Einstein stuff?"

Amanda shook her head. But she recalled the clock in the car.

"John had to accelerate to a speed that pushed his car to the limit during that last chase. He had to do it in order to save me. I remember. It was horrible. But I also remember the car rocketing across the country in seconds. The car went so fast that John couldn't control it. I had escaped the crash—or so I thought, until John talked about you. When I saw him reappear, it was a few years ago. Decades later since the accident. I had lost him." She shook her head and took a deep breath. Then she gazed at him through the window again. "I waited so long." She shook her head. "Here." She smiled ruefully at Amanda. "I never expected him to return. But, more so, I never expected you to appear too. We must have been split. One of me remained behind at the accident, the other traveled into the future. But…it's just a theory."

"I don't get it."

"Or you don't want to. You're me. You know it. But you're me decades ago. We were split by the car's jump. That's what I think happened."

"That's nuts. That would mean…all sorts of things I remember never happened in my life. But they did. I remember everything about when I was a little girl."

"Who knows from the jump," Sherry said with a shrug. "You might have somehow lived a regular life. Or the angels covered things up in your mind. There's so much we don't understand about any of their mysteries. Shit, John doesn't even know half the stuff he does as an angel. He doesn't get how that car does the stuff it does. He just knows that what he does is good."

"He thinks what he does is bad."

"He is bad." Sherry laughed. "He's real bad, Amanda. You know that. That's why you love him so much, like I do."

"He's an angel," Amanda said, shaking her head.

"He's that too." She heaved a sigh. Then she shook out her long gray hair and gestured to him. "Maybe that makes him the greatest angel of all."

"You believe John is an angel?"

She nodded.

"No, I mean, a *real* angel?"

Sherry paused. She drank some cider and looked up at the ceiling. Amanda had just wanted a quick yes or no.

"He's told me their theory. Actually, it's beautiful. The idea that we're all angels and that some are bound for heaven early. It kinda makes everyone and everything good. Even if it's not that way, even if it's somehow something else, I believe what's really out there is beautiful like that."

"I'm not so sure." Amanda sat on the bar stool. She picked up her cider again.

"Yes, I believe in angels," Sherry said with a wink. "You know why? When John made that final jump, I thought I was going to die. When we crashed, I saw a light. It shone brighter than the sun—much brighter than the light from the jumps—flooding the car, shadowing John and blotting out everything through the window. I thought it meant death. At first, it terrified me. But it was more than just light. It was brighter than the sun. And with it came a sense of such calm and ease. A feeling that no matter what's happening in this world, there will always be peace. That's beautiful too. It means that even the demons John chases are not important. It means even the devils and their evil is nothing. Even death itself is meaningless. This ride we call life ends in a chase and departure from our world, I think, a departure into that wonderful light." She shrugged. "So ever since then, yeah, I've believed very strongly in angels and God. That's the good I got from all the pain of losing him. I only see that light. All the bad does is shade us from the light of God."

And Sherry raised her glass to that and drank some more. Then she laughed. "How about you? Do you believe in angels?"

"How can I not after all that's happened."

Sherry laughed and nodded. And Amanda laughed with her.

Sherry gestured to him again. "Go to him. He won't smile. He won't nod. He'll brood. Because he's John. But inside, he's got a bigger heart than both of us. And you'll make him happy."

"It's up to him."

"Hmm, it's really not." She sipped some cider. Then she looked right into Amanda's eyes. "It's up to you. I made my decision after our recent fight in the desert. John did when he met you. Believe me, I know him." Sherry smiled. "But it will make me happy. 'Cause, Mandi, you're finally gonna make *our* John happy."

**40**

---

# MY REAL NAME

"Tony," John said, his hands deep in his jeans pockets. His eyes behind shades. He had been staring out toward the empty horizon on the desert. With his usual expressionless face. She wasn't even sure he knew she was walking up to him. "Tony's my real name, Amanda. I saw it in the deed for our place from her will."

"You want me to call you Tony, John?"

John shook his head. He turned away from Yuma and looked at her through his shades.

"She wants you to leave her for me," Amanda said.

John shook his head again. He gently took her in his arms. But then John looked over her shoulder toward Angel Dive.

Amanda turned.

Sherry stood leaning against the doorway and folding her arms, just watching them. That reminded Amanda of when she'd watched the two of them embrace when they had first entered the diner. Then she remembered the jealousy. That made her step back. But she still held his hand. And she felt him squeeze her hand tighter.

"The name's Tony," John hollered. "I saw it in the deed, Sher. Tony Lorenziano. I didn't know I was Italian."

Sherry just shrugged. Then she leaned back against the doorway.

"She never tells me a thing," John said quietly to Amanda. He removed his sunglasses and turned to her with those angel eyes. "Not a single thing. She was worried the past would hurt me because I couldn't go back. She was right. It does. I don't like being here. But I can't stay away."

"You're going with her after leaving this joint," Sherry cried out. "But the agreement includes visiting rights, John. You don't want to give me your fucking number, you better visit."

"Are you doing okay?" he asked Amanda.

"You're always asking me that."

"Are you?"

"She just told me I'm her," Amanda said with a shrug. "I *almost* believe her."

"Yeah," John said. "I've been trying to deal with it since we first met. But you act, look, and sound exactly like her." He ran a finger along her cheek. "I think she's right. I think you are her."

"She's wrong," Amanda said, shaking her head. "I remember everything from my entire life. I'm not her. What about Luane? And others I know? Hell, Mom and Dad. My entire childhood. I've known it all for years."

"They say there's a twin somewhere in this world for everyone. I don't know."

"Yeah, well, I…don't believe it." She sighed. Then she looked down. "What are we going to do?"

He gently lifted her chin and gazed at her with his naked eyes. "You've got an interview."

"Why don't you lovebirds fucking kiss each other and then get the fuck out of here!" cried Sherry, laughing heartily. "Don't worry, I'll see you back in another week,

John. Don't think you won't need your next counseling session, especially hanging with me."

"Fuck off, Sher."

He put on his shades. Then he turned to Amanda and said more quietly, "Let's go."

But Amanda let go of John's hand and ran back to the diner. Sherry flashed that tranquil smile she always gave Amanda as she approached. Then she hugged her.

"Goodbye, older-me," Amanda said.

"Goodbye, Mandi. Take care of him, okay? Take care of him for me. And take care of yourself."

"I love him."

"I love him too."

**41**

---

# CONSUMMATE SANCTUARY

John gazed at a bird soaring high and hovering over him out on the horizon. It flew down three hundred feet and quickly glided over a basin of rocks and bushes toward the horizon. The horizon was splashed a red violet as the sun was dipping down. He gazed out enjoying the view of red and violet. Beautiful.

"Angel Down," said Rick through his cell phone. "Faith. Twenty-four. An English major. Born Scorpio. She lives in Little Rock. She's traveling to a funeral in El Paso. Where you at?"

"Not far from there."

"You're still on leave," Rick said on the other end. "Intelligence tells us you've got another day before Lilith intercepts her. Leave's over."

"I'll be there."

"Hi, Rick!"

John jumped back and glared at Amanda through his shades. Amanda laughed. And seeing how serious he looked, she couldn't stop laughing.

"What the hell?" asked Rick on the line. "Is that

Sherry? Or… Amanda! Who the fuck is that? What's she doing with you?"

"I'm taking Amanda to her interview."

"Oh, fuck off, John. That's the same bullshit excuse she gave me."

"Are you feeling better?" Amanda asked, leaning over the phone.

John jerked his cell phone from her again. Then he walked to the far side of the cliff. He put the phone back against his ear. But Amanda was right behind him.

"Take her home, John," Rick said with a sigh.

"Sure."

"I mean it."

"After her interview."

"Fuck the interview. Now that Sherry's back and things are back to normal, you can get back to work."

"You said tomorrow. She'll drive me in the car to Scottsdale tonight. Then I'll help her get back home to LA after her interview. *Then* I'll take care of the one who's marked."

"Fine. Just get rid of her."

"We can't get rid of Lilith."

"I'm not talking about Lilith. Hey, wait a minute! What the hell do you mean, *she'll drive the car.*"

John hung up the phone.

He was surprised to feel Amanda take him into her arms. He turned and they kissed. He felt her body close. Their tongues danced. Then they both turned to the amazing view of the valley. The sun fell below the horizon and twilight shone forth.

"You're right, John," Amanda said, leaning on his shoulder. "This place is breathtaking."

"More breathtaking with you."

## THE END

READ THE REST OF PHANTOM HEARTS

An angel & ghost romance collection.
Each novel is a distinct standalone story.

- HAUNTING JOY
- PHANTOM MASQUERADE

The books in this series are coming soon on audiobook! Enjoy Phantom Masquerade, narrated by Caitlin Kelly; Haunting Joy and Shades coming soon.

# ALSO BY A.L. HAWKE

THE NEXT BOOKS IN THE PHANTOM HEARTS SERIES

- HAUNTING JOY
- PHANTOM MASQUERADE

URBAN FANTASY ROMANCE

- MY EVIL EYE
- THE GUARDIAN
- NECTAR OF AMBROSIA
- CORA

PARANORMAL ROMANCE

- ALONDRA
- BROOMSTICK
- WINDSTORM
- THE HAWTHORNE WITCH

FANTASY: THE AZURE SERIES TRILOGY

- CORA: RISE OF THE FALLEN GODDESS
- AZURE BLUE
- CORAL RED

SCIENCE FICTION

- CANDY SAVANT
- MOTHER SAVANT

*Books available at https://alhawke.com/books*

# PARTING WORDS

What did you think of *Shades*? By placing a book review, you can inform others of your thoughts and help spread the word about my book.

Want more? Periodically I like to send news regarding current or new projects. If you'd like to be privy, I encourage you to sign up to my email newsletter. Your information will remain private and you can cancel any time.

Sign up at www.alhawke.com or scan the following QR code:

# ACKNOWLEDGMENTS

I want to thank my beta reader George B. for helping shape this book. And to my line editor, Stephanie Marshall Ward, for the polishing and added tweaking of the story arc. To my proofreader, Alexa, for perfecting. And, finally, Regina Wamba for her artwork. John was a character in my mind long before my first book was published. I'm so happy to finally bring him out into the world.

# ABOUT THE AUTHOR

A.L. Hawke is the author of the internationally bestselling Hawthorne University Witch series. The author lives in Southern California torching the midnight candle over lovers against a backdrop of machines, nymphs, magic, spice and mayhem. A.L. Hawke writes fantasy and romance spanning four thousand years, from pre-civilization to contemporary and beyond.

Visit A.L. Hawke at www.alhawke.com

Email: contact@alhawke.com

www.ingramcontent.com/pod-product-compliance
Lightning Source LLC
Chambersburg PA
CBHW061541210726
48287CB00006B/2042